TRUSTING THE PLAYER

SMALL TOWN DESIRES #3

MISSY WALKER

Copyright © 2021 by Missy Walker

All rights reserved.

No part of this publication may be reproduced, distributed or transmitted in any form or by any means, including by any electronic or mechanical means, including photocopying, recording or information storage and retrieval systems, without prior written consent from the author, except for the use of brief quotations in a book review.

Version: 2

Cover Design: Missy Walker

Editor: Swish Design & Editing

To Mads and Viv - Break the mould and make your own rules in life x

1
AMBER

Cronuts with blood orange glaze and beetroot macaroons colored the plate like Andy Warhol art. Dessert at the newest restaurant in Seaview was definitely living up to the hype.

"Why do they call it a cronut?" Lily asked, her blue eyes seemed larger with her recent blonde pixie cut.

"It's a cross between a croissant and doughnut." Taking a bite, the Chantilly custard oozed out.

"And it's warm!" Jazzie cradled the pastry like a priceless artifact. All throughout dinner, the sound of the restaurant patrons did little to drown out Jasmine's love tentacles of happiness. If I had any emotion at all, now would be the time to feel as I watched my gorgeous friend experience a bliss unknown to me.

The girls I'd met at college had taken me in like they'd known me their entire lives, especially when I needed a friend, only I got the bonus of having two. At that time, I knew no one. Leaving my fucked-up home situation to start again in a new town wasn't easy. That's where they came in. More lifelines than friends, they were compasses who guided me, supporting me during the tumultuous time.

"Excuse me, ladies, these are for you." The waiter held a tray with three glasses of champagne.

"We didn't order any champagne," Lily said.

The waiter turned his attention from Lily to me. "Courtesy of the gentleman at the bar for you, Miss," he said, tilting his head in the direction of the bar behind him.

Me? Without waiting for a response, he placed a flute filled with pale yellow bubbles in front of me, then gave the remaining glasses to the girls.

"Thank you." I craned my neck to peer past the lanky waiter toward the bar.

Overhanging vines and wrought iron candelabras hung from the ceiling. I cast my gaze below. There, a mysterious man with dark-brown locks, tanned skin, and a body fit for an iron-man challenge, stared back at me. Any other night I'd take him home—especially since his burning stare took me to another hemisphere—but not tonight. Tonight, wasn't about me.

Jazzie turned around. "Who is that?"

"I don't know. But it doesn't matter, I'm with my girls." When I was out with my girls, I gave them my full attention. With Jazzie living in New York with Kit and Lily planning her wedding and running her own florist shop, it was rare for the three of us to get together these days. So tonight, no man, no matter how blisteringly handsome, was going to get in the way.

The waiter smiled before retreating.

"Tonight is about you, Jazzie. Lil and I are celebrating having you back in Seaview. I'm already missing you, knowing you're leaving us again so soon."

"Holy hell. Who *is* that?" Lily said, twisting her neck.

Again, as if on its own accord, my gaze shifted to him. Our eyes collide, and his lips tipped into a lopsided grin. I held up my glass and gave him a nod of appreciation for our drinks while trying to ignore the fizzle shooting up my spine.

The Adonis would have to be put on ice...

Forcing myself to look away once again, I returned my attention back on my girls, but Jazzie's stare remained on him.

"Oh, he's coming over." Jazzie whipped her head back around, her eyes as wide as the half-eaten cronuts in front of us. "Damn, girl, he is handsome." She giggled.

Thundering palpitations knocked at my chest with each step he drew nearer to our table. He sauntered across the busy restaurant floor, his almond-shaped eyes glued to mine.

"Good evening, ladies," he said through a wide smile. His voice, rich like mahogany, was almost as tempting as his scent of cinnamon and cedarwood invading my nostrils. Dark, well-kept stubble adorned his square jaw and catlike green-blue eyes sidelined me more than I'd like to admit.

"Hi!" Jazzie and Lily said in unison, like the choir from *Sister Act*.

Smiling, he returned his focus to me. "You're welcome."

He had the kind of hair you'd love to run your hands through, long on top with tapered sides. I swallowed. *How long has it been?*

"Thanks for the drinks, but as you can see, we are having a girls' night."

"I can see that," he said, his cemented stance unshakable.

I tilted my chin. "So, that means, no men."

"Is that a rule you have?" he asked.

"Rule?" Lily interjected. "Amber loves her rules."

"Amber." His glare, prey-like and unmoving, sent pulses between my thighs.

Raising an eyebrow, I questioned, "Can you take a hint, Casanova, or are you as arrogant as your good looks?"

Lily laughed and Jazzie covered her mouth, but he didn't show any reaction. He stood, unperturbed. Dressed in casual jeans and a crisp baby-blue shirt with the sleeves rolled up, you'd be mistaken to think he fit in if it wasn't for his expensive tan loafers.

I crossed my legs under the table. His arrogance wasn't like the other twenty-somethings that tried it on. Where others would have scampered, he stayed, unfazed by my rebuttal—like he knew he would win, as if he always got what he wanted.

My skin hummed from my neck down. *No, not tonight.*

"I'll be at the bar, when you change your mind." He smiled, and at this distance, it revealed a set of movie-star teeth.

"And they say whales have enormous balls!" Lily licked the macaroon crumb that dotted her mouth.

"Ah, Mr. Full of Himself is pretty damn gorgeous, though. Right, Amber?" Jazzie asked.

"Sure, he is. And any other night, I'd probably take him home and lose myself in him, but—"

"And then what? Don't get his number because of your rules?"

"You know my rules keep me safe. What I was going to say before you cut me off, but I won't, because how often do I get to see you both now? Our weekly dinners have been non-existent since you moved to New York, Jazzie." I took another bite of the cronut. "And, Lily, you're busy with your new florist shop… which, by the way, is so gorgeous."

"Look who's talking! You've been working around the clock. Trying to reach you is impossible. I have more luck when I'm in New York than when I'm here. At least I know you'll be up in the middle of the night working when it's the a.m. in Manhattan."

"True, but when you love what you do, it's not really a job." Jazzie arched an eyebrow. "I know Skype isn't the same, but I'm here now and let's just enjoy…" she flicked her wrist, "… the half hour left before I have to get to the airport."

"We can't keep the famous rock star waiting," Lily joked. Truth was, Kit and his band, Four Fingers, were exploding on the charts worldwide, and he couldn't be a nicer guy with a nicer girl than Jasmine.

"Kit said he'd meet me at JFK. How sweet is that?"

"Sugary sweet," I said. I was happy for her, truly. But we were wired differently. For starters, I didn't do relationships. After what I witnessed growing up, I firmly gave myself two rules. I lived by them and never strayed. With a subtle quick shake of my head to clear my thoughts, I focused on my friend and her happiness.

She grinned. "I told you I'm joining him on tour for a while, didn't I?"

"Yes, how exciting! What a trip that would be."

Lily wrapped her fingers around the last macaroon as she gave me a pointed look. "You know, Amber, he's still looking at you."

I glanced over our round table toward the bar.

He sat on the oak stool, leaning against the bar opposite a woman, seemingly oblivious to her conversation. The dim lighting did zero to shadow the lust-filled energy shared between us. He was staring directly at me, while simultaneously chatting someone up, who from the way she was stroking his bicep, appeared to be a sure thing.

Who does that? Someone with moon-sized cajones and a gold-plated schlong, that's who, and it sent a flutter to my core.

"I'm going to miss you guys so much. Please come to New York and visit me and Kit. There's a ticket there waiting for you," Jazzie said.

"I can get my own ticket," I said.

"Of course, you can." Jazzie smiled. She'd known me long enough to know I didn't mean to offend her.

"Summer in New York sounds amazing, maybe I could

convince Blake," Lily said, a smile spilling across her cheeks. God, could my besties be any more in love? *Ugh.*

"Just think about it, girls," Jazzie added.

I downed the rest of my double espresso—the hot liquid sliding down my throat. It would aid in my midnight research on Magma Gold. Starting tomorrow, under my boss's supervision, I'd be the youngest lawyer in the firm I worked for— Jackson and Lane Lawyers— to be heading up a merger. And not just any merger. Magma Gold was the firm's most prestigious client. I'd already done a ton of research, but I didn't get in this position by doing what every other associate had done before me. Hell no. I had goals and held myself to a higher standard.

It was just after ten when we exited the restaurant, but it still buzzed with a mixture of backpackers and wealthy holiday makers. In under three years, Seaview had transformed from a local coastal town an hour from Brisbane to a tourist mecca where people flocked like seagulls, taking five different photos to try to capture the perfect Instagram-worthy shot. And to accommodate the new money, trendy bars and restaurants had been popping up more frequently than pimples on a teenage boy.

"Bye, gals," Jazzie said as the taxi pulled up.

I clawed her in for a bear hug. "I hope it's not this long between drinks next time."

She hugged me tightly, and to prevent a too long of a goodbye, I let go first. Long hugs reminded me of Mom, and then the guilt came thick and fast.

"Let's FaceTime next week," Jazzie suggested.

"Definitely."

Lily hugged Jazzie for a long time, their close friendship evident. "Lil, if you don't let her go, she'll miss her flight." Gently, I peeled Lily's bear grip she had around Jazzie's shoulders.

"Love you both," she said, with glassy eyes.

I closed the door to the taxi. "Love you too!" Lily and I both said in unison.

The cab pulled away, taking our best friend back to New York, to the man of her dreams, and her new life.

I turned to Lily, her eyes glossy. "I'm okay," she sniffled.

I put my arm around her shoulders. "I know you are."

I peered down at her jacket flopped over her handbag. "Dammit."

"What's wrong?" She glanced up at me.

"I left my jacket in the restaurant."

"You're so forgetful," Lily said.

With a shake of my head I agreed. " I think I'm just tired."

"Want me to come back in with you?"

"No, go. If you're lucky you'll make it home before the rain sets in."

She wrapped her arms around me, and I gave her a big squeeze. "Dinner next week?" she asked, gathering her jacket above her head, catching the spits of rain that fell from the blackened sky.

"Absolutely."

I made a beeline into the restaurant, instantly spotting the denim jacket draped along the back of the oak chair. I scooped it up, turned around, and automatically set my focus on the bar, scouring it for the face that made me feel *something*. But he wasn't there, nor was the woman he'd been sitting with. I darted toward the exit, pushing open the heavy glass door and inhaled a lungful of crisp, wet air. I let out a low grumble as I set about the shortcut via the alleyway, annoyed with myself for letting any man affect me in that way.

"Hey." He appeared from the shadows. If it wasn't for his smooth voice, the same one that hadn't left me since dinner, I'd have taken off quicker than Usain Bolt.

He was tall, at least a head taller than me, strong, fit, and as his eyes lingered from mine to my lips, and I heated instantly. His gaze set me alight. His arrogance, top of the charts, and a hell of a turn-on. He knew what he wanted and admittedly, so did I.

"Hey, yourself." My legs stopped, obeying the deep need I had within and ignored the endless research awaiting me in my apartment. "Where's your muse?"

"She's right in front of me."

"Am I?" I bit my lip. "I was hoping you'd say that."

Leaning in, he grinned, and I took a hesitant step back, hitting the brick wall lining the alleyway. His chin was only inches from mine, and his breath whispered against my mouth. My heart pounded. This was what I wanted right now, right here—forget work, forget friends, forget life. It was becoming a routine, wrapping myself up in men to forget it all. I'd stop it soon—probably—but I needed him now.

His full, thick lips pressed to mine, taking them like a life raft. His tongue raked my lower teeth and his body pressed against mine as the mortar dug into my back. His knees spread my legs apart, his thickness on my thigh. *Fuck*, this guy was hot, dark, and dangerous with eyes that pulled me in to his web.

"We can't do this here," I breathed.

Suddenly, he grabbed my hand and ran, which left me no choice but to grip his hand. Nearly tripping over my heels, I stepped in and around puddles, the water splashing on my ankles. I ran beside him, like school kids itching to skip class, following him down the alleyway, where pedestrian light faded into gray, and the bitumen was slick from the rain.

The thought of taking him to my place left as quick as it came. This was *way* hotter. The rain fell, shooting down from the sky and wetting my emerald dress. He stopped when we reached an alcove of crates as high as a two-story building. He pinned me behind the wall of timber, hoisted me up with one arm, and automatically my legs wrapped around his waist. My breast spilled out of my bra, and he buried his head into my chest. He grazed my nipple with his teeth, eliciting the perfect amount of pain and pleasure.

"Aghh," I let out, his touch exploding inside me.

"Don't you want to know my name?" he groaned as he abandoned my nipple to look at me.

I pushed my mouth to his and kissed him hard, then withdrew. "You're not a local. Or a backpacker. Which means you're here on business. Either way, I won't see you after tonight, so, no."

"I think I've met my match," he answered almost as breathlessly as me. The rain sheeted around us, soaking my dress—it clung to me like a second skin. Balancing me, he undid his jeans, freeing his erection. With the other hand, he reached into a pocket and pulled out a foil packet. He tore it open and, still holding me, managed to wrap himself, all while his almond eyes bored into mine.

"What are you waiting for?" I asked.

A crack of lightning lit up the sky, his dark eyes glinted mysteriously and lava hot. He pushed my lace underwear to the side and entered me swiftly with two fingers, back and forth, pleasuring me to the nth degree. I shuddered with his touch. Then, without any warning, he removed his fingers and entered me with his full thick erection. Filling me perfectly, every thrust gave me pleasure I'd never experienced. I threw my head back as he cradled me in his arms. My breasts bobbed up and down as he buried his face into them, his beard grazing them.

"Fuck," he hissed, continuing his heady invasion.

His hot breath clothed my skin. I took his mouth to mine, and he deepened the kiss, his tongue dancing with mine. I clawed at his shirt, feeling his broad shoulders and steel-clad muscles. My own body coiled with pleasure in response.

Unable to hold onto the explosive feeling building inside of me, I let out a moan.

Again, he took his lips to mine, his rough stubble no doubt leaving its mark. At this point, he could brand me. I didn't care. My thighs quaked, taking in all the pleasure until it became overwhelming. My nails dug into him tighter. "Shit," I blew out, finding my release.

Holy hell.

My legs were heavy, but he didn't let me go. He groaned as he thrust a few more times, then found his release. "Fuck!"

2

LOGAN

My brother, Carlton, stood in his corner office and stared out the window on the twenty-eighth floor, his hands in his charcoal Armani suit pockets. His combed-over salt and pepper hair barely covered his balding patch.

Walking into his opulent office, he's completely oblivious to my presence with his back to me. Situated halfway between the Gold Coast and Brisbane were the Magma headquarters. Similar to the Gherkin in London, shards of glass wrapped the building, obtuse in its enormity. Commissioned by Daddio, of course, not Gammy and Pop who stepped aside over twenty-five years ago.

I cleared my throat because he obviously didn't know I was standing here.

Letting out an audible huff, he turned to look at me and gave a slight shake of his head in irritation.

Hey, brother." Even the word *brother* came off sarcastically.

"Look who's here." Carlton glared at his gold Rolex. "You're three minutes late."

"Sue me."

"Be late again and I just might."

"Three minutes. Seriously? I had a late night in Seaview... not that I owe you an explanation."

"Where?"

"Seaview," I tsked. Heck, Carlton ought to climb back under the rock he came from. "The coastal town that's a hidden gem along the Queensland coastline."

He thinned his eyes and walked from the corner window to his desk, where he picked up a file.

I dug my hands into my pant pockets. Trying to make conversation with my only sibling was worse than nails on a chalkboard. "It's about an hour from here," I blew out.

"I wouldn't know. I'm too busy running a billion-dollar mining company."

Magma, a third-generation gold mining company, is now firmly the largest gold mining company in Australia. Over the last decade, it had grown exponentially, contributing over three hundred ounces of gold per annum in the last five years alone. Funnily enough, that tidbit of information hadn't come from Daddy dearest—I'd read it in the *Financial Review* on the first-class flight home from Barcelona.

Stamps filled my passport pages, and in the last decade, those countries were more of a home to me than I'd ever had. With me on the other side of the world, their problem child was out of sight, Carlton and Dad focused on taking Pop's mid-tier gold mining company into the stratosphere, all while I was getting lost in whitewashed alleyways of Andalusia or lazing on a superyacht off the coast of Ibiza.

"Well, I was busy getting laid."

He shook his head. "Doesn't that get old?"

"Just to clarify, you're asking me if sex with gorgeous random women gets old? Did you take your pills this morning?"

He rolled his eyes. "At some point, you have to grow up."

"Why? I'm staring at you and see a thirty-five-year-old man who resembles a fifty year old you."

"And I'm looking at you, Logan and I see a twenty-five-year-old little boy who is in jeopardy of being thrown out of the family fortune unless he can prove himself and grow the fuck up."

"Well, someone forgot to ejaculate this morning."

"Fuck you, Logan."

"You know that helps with the tension of a big day." I tried not to smirk. I really did. Okay, that's an overstretch. I wanted him to see my ear-splitting grin.

He banged his fist on the table. "Madeleine," he yelled for his secretary.

I walked across the timber flooring, taking the farthest chair from Carlton's throne behind his desk. Sinking into the cream-colored leather high-back chair, I stared out toward the cloudless sky.

Fuck! Why was I even here?

Cloaked in Amber's scent from last night, I still swam in the shrine of a woman who'd shown me more sass and connection than any before her. And that included my on-and-off again, society hanger-on, Celia. When I had to make the punishing trip back to Australia a few times a year for the holidays, Ceila was always there—a presence at family balls and important dinners. She was the perfect partner from a blue-blooded political family, and my parents adored her—another reason I didn't. *Amber* didn't need my name. Hadn't wanted it. She didn't seem the of love 'em and leave 'em kind of girl. But then, as quick as she gripped my heart, she let go. Without a trace, without a phone number. Others would judge her for her actions. Not me. I welcomed it. There wasn't anything distasteful about last night, only fucking magic.

"Madeleine!" Carlton yelled louder this time, his face glowing red. The three of us had taken the private jet from

Perth to Brisbane, and I saw how he treated her firsthand. What a fuck-hole. I swear he got off on being a dick to not only her but anyone who appeared beneath him. And in Carlton's eyes, that was everyone.

I turned, and she appeared in the door frame. "Sorry, sir, I didn't hear you. What can I do for you?"

"Get me the files on the Danker deal." He kept his eyes on his desk, not bothering to look up.

"Are you forgetting the magic word, Carlton?" I tossed Madeleine a wink, and she blinked. A few weeks ago, we'd both ended up at a bar drunk and back at her place. And ever since, she'd appeared flustered whenever I was around.

Carlton tilted his head up and glared. If looks could kill, his was a psycho killer with a machete about to slice and dice me.

"Yes, yes, of course, I'll bring it in now." Madeleine cut through the silence as she side-glanced me before darting from the room.

"Never try to undermine me again in front of anyone," he snapped. "Now, Logan, I don't need to remind you about the importance of this meeting."

"Who are we buying again?"

"Are you fucking kidding me? You're a goddamn joke. I don't know why Mom and Dad wanted you in. I could handle this merger myself with my eyes closed."

"Well, if it makes you feel any better, I don't want to be here just as much as you don't want me here."

"Doubtful. If this were some kind of joke, they would have called it now." He checked his phone. "Nope, nothing from Mom or Dad. Why would they pull this shit on me? Don't they know I'm running the empire?"

"Sounds like the joke is on you then?" I grinned, enjoying the pain inflicted on my perfect brother.

Yeah, I see the humor in it all, too, brother. Since graduating from Rowley College, the elite English boarding school I sent away to, my life had been a mixture of random sex, society parties, yachts in Greece, and waking up to a new adventure each day. But no. Not anymore. They had cut my allowance and threatened my trust fund. Now, I had to come to work in the family business.

He sighed, exasperation strewn on his face. "Danker Gold, ever heard of them?"

"Maybe?"

"Small-cap gold company in North Queensland. We are buying them. Do the proper due diligence. I've outlined everything in the files. Let me know if there are any discrepancies in the preliminaries. You've got the support from our local legal and accounting firms, both in Queensland. Relay between the two and just get it done. Clear?"

"As mud."

He narrowed his eyes, his forehead wrinkled into a patch of lines.

"Try to search for a brain in there somewhere, Logan. Because after we meet with the law firm this morning, I'm flying back to Perth, and all this is on your shoulders. This is a fifty-million-dollar deal, but the upside is five times that. Do the sums and lead your team." He shook his head.

"Use that expensive private schoolboy education."

"Which one are you referring to? Where my lovely parents hoarded me off to carry out my schooling in the strictest boarding school in London or the Oxford degree in fine arts?"

"Both, but then again, you never finished it, so I don't know if you've got the brains to do this?"

Mom seems to think you do. Dad and I, well, we don't want to squash her last hope of you. Her twenty-six-year-old son with zero direction in life, zero ideas and no hope, no dreams and goals, and living off swimming around Mommy and Daddy's inheritance."

"Oh, you got it. That's me to a tee. You're on point today. Did Madeleine blow you before your morning coffee?"

"Sorry to interrupt, but I have the documents you requested." Madeleine approached his desk.

"Next time, don't interrupt," he snapped.

"For your information, I've been faithful to my wife. Monogamy, try it sometime."

"Sure, you have." I looked at him with an arched brow of skepticism.

He grabbed the files Madeleine placed on his desk. "Let's go. The car is waiting, and if I stay here any longer, I think I'll deck you."

A laugh escaped me. "I think you're confusing me with a soft toy. There's nothing soft about me."

He let out an exasperated sigh. "Don't push me, Logan."

I'd returned to Australia because my family had asked me to, but I didn't need to put up with this. "Or what?"

He flung around the desk, quicker than lightning, his nostrils flaring.

"Or I'll make sure you don't see a square cent of your inheritance."

I stared at him. The fucker would too. I didn't doubt him for a second.

3

AMBER

Last night was intense. In an alleyway in Seaview, I'd given another stranger my virtue.

I had my two rules.

Rule One—Never sleep with the same man twice.

Rule Two—Never mix business and pleasure.

Lily and Jazzie knew my rules, and they didn't judge. Why would they? If men could sleep around and not get name shamed, so could women.

We all had needs, and usually, I took care of my own, taking home a one-night stand here and there. Even then, I'd still have to take matters into my own hands if I wanted any satisfaction. That is, until last night. He'd been the first to give me the *big O* outside of myself. And the first to make me think twice about the two rules I lived by.

Outdoor sex wasn't my style, but the draw of his eyes and the touch of his words rendered me helpless. The way he effortlessly held me, pushing me against the wall, gave me unearthly chills. The scratches on my lower back, still raw a day later, a reminder of the confident-as-hell man with tantric eyes and golden touch.

I stepped inside the fluorescent-lit elevator and pressed the button to the third-floor offices of Chadwick Lane Lawyers, trying to suppress the heat spreading from my shoulders upward to my neck and cheeks.

Whoa! Think of something else, Amber. Now is not the time.

The doors pinged open, and I smoothed down my skirt before stepping out. Empty cubicles stood on the maroon nylon carpeted office. I marched past the desks toward the corner cubicle with the hanging sign, *Amber Anderson*. Surrounded by senior associates and the partners, Chadwick Ward and Theodore Lane, I was the only junior with a desk at this end of the office.

Arriving early is what I did. It didn't yield me any favor amongst my colleagues, nor did my recent desk change, but I couldn't care less. The not-so-subtle whispers calling me *brown-noser* and *bootlicker* when I'd walked past the water cooler did nothing but put a charge in my step. They didn't know my situation or why I tried my damndest.

"Good morning, Amber." Chadwick Lane peeked up from his laptop. His gold-framed round glasses rested halfway down his bulbous nose. Turning sixty last week didn't stop Chadwick arriving to work first, something I admired about the mentor he'd become to me over the last five years of working for him.

I stood in the door frame and returned the greeting, "Morning, Chadwick. I'm excited about today and thank you for trusting me to handle the due diligence on this takeover." I said, as I gripped the leather handles on my chestnut briefcase.

"Sit down, please, Amber."

"Okay." I sat on one of the two teak armchairs opposite him.

"I chose you to lead this merger because of your persistence and commitment. You showed me that when I met you at age eighteen and turned you down for a job here."

"I remember that day clearly." My new friends, Lily and

Jasmine, had called me crazy for applying for a graduate position two weeks into my four-year law degree, but I didn't see it that way.

"Well, your constant stalking and nagging the weeks after I turned you down got you in the door here."

"I wouldn't say stalking." I grinned.

"Five years ago, you lived in Seaview…"

"Still do."

"And JJ's Café is next door to our offices… not exactly in your neck of the woods."

"They make a delicious latte, what can I say?" I smiled, remembering the daily trudge I'd made to JJ's Café and waited out front for Chadwick to appear because I'd spent what little money I had to get here. I soon realized he listened better to my repeated requests for a job once he'd taken a few sips.

"Well, I'm glad you hustled me. Since then, you've shown your dedication and your unwavering support to this firm, putting in hours beyond your requirements."

"Thank you for noticing."

"You're more direct than an arrow, Amber. Now, this merger is with one of our longest-standing clients. They know what they want, and anything less than perfection is not good enough."

"I've read everything there is on Carlton Magma and Magma Gold, including the preliminary documents on their takeover with Danker Gold."

"Good. So you know, Magma Gold is one of the fastest-growing gold mining companies in Australia. They have gained over two billion dollars' worth of acquisitions in the last decade, and they are a family business who are very close. This merger, although on a smaller scale than their previous acquisitions, is being run by Carlton himself. You will travel with Carlton and the accountants from the Rothplan Accountancy firm."

"Understood." Repeating himself had become all too common. I could be doing so much more work right now than listening to this again.

"Now you know that this could be anywhere from a few days up to a week. I don't expect it to be more than that, but we are at the client's will here, and they want things done one hundred and ten percent. Carlton is meticulous."

As he spoke, my mind wandered to last night's alleyway tryst. The R-rated movie looped in my head. The hot rain drenched his cotton shirt, so it clung to his riptide of torso muscles. His wet, full lips were firm and possessive when he claimed mine. The flashing skyline and falling rain, the perfect setting for a romantic movie. I blinked rapidly, the words romantic and Amber didn't belong in the same sentence. I only needed to look to my family lineage to see that catastrophe.

"Amber?"

"Yes. Sorry. I've done my research on Magna, I've packed my bag, and I'm ready. You can count on me."

The morning disappeared quicker than Swiss cheese in a mousetrap. I stared at the files I'd alphabetized and knew inside out. I couldn't be more across this merger if I'd tried.

I checked my watch. With ten minutes before our noon meeting, I reclined to the sound of buzzing phones, low voices, and keyboard warriors. Closing my eyes, I immersed myself in the memory of the man from last night.

"Amber, are you unwell?" I startled, opening my eyes. Chadwick appeared by the side of my cubicle. His blue eyes had sunk, his frown lines deeper than I'd recalled.

"No, sir, I'm perfectly fine. Thank you."

Gemma, Chadwick's new secretary, suddenly appeared behind him. Her perfume hit like blunt-force trauma.

"Gemma?" I welcomed the intrusion rather than having to explain my out-of-character absent-mindedness to Chadwick.

"Chadwick. I have Carlton Sagma and his associates to see

you. They're in the boardroom." She flashed me her best fake smile on sumo lips pumped full of shit before sweeping her hair over her shoulder when Chadwick turned. We had nothing in common, and we both knew it. She craved attention, I craved quiet. She got a job through Daddy. I actually worked my ass off to get here. She's the first I'd vote out on *Survivor*.

"It's Carlton *Magma*, not *Sagma*. Thank you, Gemma."

"Right." She turned on her heel as Chadwick cranked his head around and rolled his eyes.

"I wish Maggie hadn't retired," he said.

"Me too."

"Make us shine, Amber."

"I won't do anything less than my best," I said, fixing my gaze on the weathered man.

He nodded. I got up, smoothed down my black skirt, collected my documents, and walked beside him toward the boardroom.

A flicker of trepidation pulsed throughout my body. For the first time in a long time, nerves gnawed at my stomach. Chadwick had chosen me, rather than a senior associate, to go to the mine and head up the due diligence for the merger. But I knew, even though I'd worked my tail off to get here, it was only a stepping stone to bigger and better things. The promise of a bigger salary and the title of senior associate—all the things I'd worked so hard to achieve were now within reach. Strange, how only a few years ago, I didn't even know if I could escape my home. Yet, here I was heading up a merger, leaving behind the scared girl, the one who stood helpless as she watched her mother getting beat up by her father.

"Here we go," Chadwick said, sliding open the mahogany double doors. I walked in and lifted my head. Suddenly, I froze. Across the boardroom table, the same smoky gray eyes from the alleyway stared back at me. Confusion spun through my head like a web as my feet stood cemented to the carpeted floor. *What was he doing here?* But by his gray eyes the size of tires, he wasn't expecting to see me either. Words escaped me, and all I heard were the muffled greetings of the other men.

My gaze lingered on the man from the alleyway as I tried to unjumble my p's from my q's.

"Amber?" I whipped my head around. Chadwick's bushy eyebrows pulled down together into a scowl.

"Yes, I'm Amber Anderson, pleasure to meet you, Mr. Magma." I quickly extended my hand toward Carlton Magma, the CEO of Magma I'd recognized from my research.

"So, you're the one Chadwick harps on about." He took my hand and shook it like a limp leaf.

I smiled. "I guess so."

"This is my brother, Logan. You'll be working with him on this."

Logan.

I swallowed just enough to keep my heart from exploding out of my chest.

Logan stood, clad in an expensive-looking navy suit with a crisp white shirt. He looked different than his jeans and shirt from the night before. Well-kept dark brown hair wasn't falling down his rain-soaked face. It was coiffed to perfection and strand perfect like the stubble that dotted his sharp jawline.

I extended my hand. "Nice to meet you, Logan," I said, trying to keep my head from spinning and hitting the floor.

He paused, staring at me with those smoky eyes, and my breath hitched in my throat. *Say nothing. Say nothing, Logan. Please.* He took my hand in his—soft but firm like the balance of restraint he showed last night. "Pleasure to meet you, Amber."

Carlton took his seat, and we all followed his lead. I wracked my brain. Nowhere in my research had it said Carlton had a brother. I opened the binders and documents in front of me, trying to click back into some semblance of professionalism. But as I did, I could feel his gaze across the room without even having to look at him. Every hair stood on its end.

This is not happening. Focus, Amber.

"Right, let's get straight to it. I have a plane on standby to take me back to Perth. Danker Gold owns an old gold mine in Bundaberg, which we have yet to gain. The CEOs are awaiting your arrival," Carlton said to Logan and me.

My laser focus hovered on Carlton, even though a magnetic force kept a grip on me. Automatically, my thighs pressed together underneath the table.

"There is a list in the documents of research on the leasehold arrangement we need to check. The tenure with the state and local governments and the agreements in play are to be cross-referenced with what we have agreed to."

"Senators and their contacts are in the binder at the federal level."

"So, we aren't going through the regular Queensland government channel?" I piped up.

"No, Amber. And if I have to repeat everything twice, this will take twice as long."

What an ass. I heated from my feet up, burning under the surface. That was a reasonable question I wanted to say but kept quiet.

"My brother lacks the so-called manners we all seem to have," Logan said.

I blinked rapidly. Did he just defend me?

His brother, however, shot daggers at him. "To be young and naïve."

Chadwick laughed, and I glanced at him sideways. I didn't need anyone to come to my defense, but for my mentor to laugh? The light that surrounded Chadwick dimmed for the first time since I knew him.

"It's been too long, Carlton, so long in fact, I even forgot you had a brother. No disrespect, Logan."

Logan peered up from his phone at the mention of his name, then returned to the glow in his hands.

"Speaking of, from our correspondence, Carlton, I thought you were heading to Bundaberg with Amber," Chadwick commented.

"Logan's been gallivanting around the world and only recently returned, so he can handle this."

I focused on Logan. The man seemed oblivious to the meeting taking place before his very eyes.

"Logan?" Carlton's booming voice cut like a knife. It was enough for his younger brother to put down his smartphone and recline into his seat, folding his arms over his chest.

"Is there something on your phone that needs your attention right this minute?" Carlton pressed.

Logan turned to his brother, his jaw set. "Not on my phone, specifically." He turned toward me. "But things need my attention." The corner of his mouth curled into a smirk.

I felt the color drain from my face. Tilting my head, I buried it into the papers in front of me. *Three seconds in and breathe. And exhale.* While the others spoke, I did rounds of breathing, trying to regain my faculties from the powerful puppeteer sitting opposite me.

The meeting continued for the next hour, and I held my poise like Lady Liberty. Well, I certainly tried. Deflecting the waves of attention and sparks of lust Logan aimed my way became more difficult with each minute that passed. I prayed Chadwick and Carlton didn't pick up on the innuendo because, if they did, my trip to Bundaberg and the promise of a fat bonus wouldn't happen. *And I needed that.*

"So that's it. Amber, you can chat with my secretary, Madeleine, about your travel arrangements. She's waiting for you outside." Carlton smiled at me, and I felt slightly relieved. Over the course of the meeting, my few but direct questions may have won him over. If you could, in fact, win over Carlton.

I got out of my head for a minute and nodded. "Yes, absolutely."

"So, I'm jetting back to Perth today. If you've got any issues, Amber, speak to Logan, and if he can't answer them, speak to me." He handed me his business card. I ran my fingers over the crisp linen and gold embossed card. *Fitting*.

Logan huffed under his breath, and Carlton threw him a fiery stare. What was the deal between those two?

"Thank you, Carlton. I'm sure you're very busy, so between the three of us, I'm sure we'll manage."

"At least someone realizes what it takes to run a multi-million-dollar business." Carlton rose to his feet.

Logan smirked. "Don't you worry, dear brother. Amber and I will get to the bottom of this merger."

I pushed my seat out and stood, turning my back to him and hiding the blush that crept up my neck. *How could he be so obvious?* Did he even care about this merger? Well, he had another thing coming. Magma was our client, and if Logan wasn't interested in this deal, it was up to me to ensure Magma had the best representation possible without him getting in my way.

4
LOGAN

Well, thank the fucking stars. This merger wouldn't suck dick after all. Stuck together for the foreseeable future, Amber, the insatiable woman with her chignon bun and murder-red lips, might just make this thing called work bearable.

I half-listened as they discussed the Heads of Agreement, assets, and the many other details I tuned out during the mundane meeting. Enduring the musty-scented board room had become tolerable the more I zeroed in on *her* and the more she tried avoiding me.

Just ten hours earlier and under the crescent moon, her lips sucked at my neck while her hands fisted my hair. And now, it gave me pleasure watching her writhe in the leather seat as my gaze fell upon her. Heck, I had to distract myself and scan my phone just to take my mind off the semi that lengthened in my suit pants. But as the meeting ended, the differences between the Amber of last night and the Amber who sat opposite me became more apparent by the minute. The problem was the innate attraction I had to both. She definitely looked the lawyer part, her intelligent questions surprising even the stalest of them all, Carlton. I could tell because, after a while, he let up on her and started listening rather than talking down like he always did.

Brains and beauty, all put together nicely. Incredibly nice. Except, in this environment, she was passive, almost malleable, like Play-Doh.

Was that just corporate life? Did it suck the life out of everyone or just Amber?

I craved the sassy girl from the restaurant with the shoulder-length, smooth brown hair and the forest-green dress with a thigh split that showed off her slender olive-skinned legs. The girl who sat opposite me had the same sultry hazel eyes but yielded to any boss's requests because they held her career in their dirty hands.

"I'd like a word with Chadwick." Carlton sat back down and glared in my direction. "Join Amber outside."

"As you wish, boss." I saluted the dick, and I could feel the steam billowing out of Carltons' ears. Toying with him gave me shrills of pleasure. Now, coupled with my new muse on this project, I was in wonderland.

After I slid the timber doors shut, I walked toward the foyer. Amber walked ahead of me and toward Madeleine, her black skirt clinging to her pert ass. Momentarily, I took my eyes off her behind and took in the godforsaken shitstorm of offices that desperately needed a refurbishment.

Why Carlton chose a law firm that would fit right at home on a Nevada strip was beyond me. It wasn't a firm I'd choose. If they couldn't spend money making their firm look barely presentable, how could they run a proper shop? But apparently, they'd been doing business together for years.

When Carlton said we had a meeting with the lawyers on the East Coast, I had in mind a Brisbane skyscraper—multiple floors, clean lines, and angled furniture. Not a small, three level firm on the outskirts of Brisbane and in a building that needed repointing and serious odor removal. The smell was so bad, it was as though a disgruntled ex-employee had flung up some prime rib in the ceiling cavity just as a *fuck you* on their way out.

But hell, I wasn't in charge. I'd never be, nor did I want to. Why even offer a suggestion? I learned a long time ago that it wasn't my place, and it was a wasted energy.

Amber drew her chair in and adjusted her skirt as it bunched against her thighs. She pulled her worn blazer closed like she knew I was watching her. *Honey, I've seen it all before.* Her golden skin, smooth and desperate on mine under the moonlight. I felt a stare as I sat down beside her, shifting my attention to Madeleine's icy glare fired at me like falling stalactites.

"Hello, you must be Madeleine," Amber said.

I watched the two women as they conversed. Madeleine with her blonde hair and petite frame who turned heads, but Amber had me hooked. I wasn't sure if it was because of her long legs and piercing hazel eyes or the fact I hadn't stopped thinking about her since the alleyway.

If only I could sneak a quick word with Amber, torturing her even more. *Oh God, this was going to be fun.* Exhilaration punched through my veins.

"Mmmaddie." I rolled my lips together stressing the *M* as I leaned on the cheap wooden table she sat behind. She looked at me like all the other women did. Or rather, past me, into the possible life the Magma last name offered. The gold-diggers were more obvious than fake diamonds. She batted the eyelashes she had stuck on. Okay, so sleeping with her probably wasn't my best decision, but screw it, anything to piss my brother off. Or, perhaps now, I could use it to make Amber jealous.

"Logan, your accommodation information is here. You're staying at a beautiful place, just like you requested. You will have a driver on standby. I've organized all of that. But I couldn't get a local chef for you…" She bit her lip. "I hope that's okay. It happened so quickly... you coming into the company... then being in control of this merger. It all happened way too fast for me to take care of every aspect."

Madeleine flushed ruby red. She wasn't talking about the merger.

A slight smirk spread onto Amber's face. She wasn't at all intimidated. Not a smidge jealousy. Perhaps, I had met my match.

Madeleine cleared her throat. "So, the mine is in the middle of nowhere. I've scouted the nearest restaurants for you, Logan, but they are scant. Really, there isn't much on offer except for burgers and chips, which I know is definitely not adequate." She flicked her blonde hair behind her ear. "I'm still scouting around to find a chef for you. However, I'll have to fly someone to the site. So I'm waiting on a sign-off from your brother on that. I'm so sorry it's not organized yet," she rambled on.

"So, I have to go out for my meals?" Amber stared at me, her jaw ajar. *Pick it up, sweetheart, or you know what you can do with it.* "Scouting for a meal after a hard day's work is the last thing I want to do."

"Absolutely, Logan. I just haven't been able to find anyone that can fly out on such short notice and have the ability to cook what you like."

"And what is it you like?" Amber shot up an eyebrow.

"Are we talking about food?" I smirked.

"Yes, of course," she hurled back.

"I enjoy caviar... beluga, pate, wagyu steak, steak tartare. And you?"

"I don't have a preference." She stopped short of saying anything more, but why did I get the feeling she wasn't finished?

News flash. Raised with nannies, servants, and anything else I wanted, I was adequately spoiled. But being spoiled meant different things to different people. Parent favoritism and being shipped off to another country at thirteen years old was anything but.

"Well, I guess you'll just have to get accustomed to the Queensland hospitality rather than private chefs. That could be a challenge, but I'm sure you'll get there." Amber's voice was a trifle of sarcasm and disdain.

This was going to be a ball. Even though she'd probably woken the residents in the street last night with her very vocal orgasm, she hated me with a passion. It stirred something for me.

She took this whole work thing way too seriously. Why? I had no idea. I'd never known anyone so driven before. I planned to use it to my advantage. She could run this deal, and I could sit back. *Perfect.*

Madeleine looked back and forth between Amber and me. "Do you know each other?"

"No," Amber said quickly. "What makes you say that?"

"Oh nothing, sorry. I should mind my own business."

Madeleine looked from me to Amber, jealousy in her eyes.

"Where am I staying?" Amber asked. "Don't worry about me, I don't need any special chefs or fancy accommodation. I'm a single girl from a simple coastal town."

At this, I roared into laughter. She must think I'm a bigger prick than a paddle cactus. "So, you don't enjoy the fancy things?"

She cleared her throat. "Nope, I don't. I'm perfectly fine as I am. But thank you for asking, Logan." She eyed me. The heat between us was undeniable. She had me beyond melting with a simple glance.

"I'd like a word, Amber," I said.

"Sure," Amber said, unfazed by my request.

Trying to keep pace with her, I followed Amber while I

ignored Madeleine's stare piercing holes into the back of my navy, Tom Ford suit.

"Step into my office," she said, arm extended and showing me into a high-walled cubicle with no doors. I glanced around—the nearest person was at least ten yards away.

She sat down on the edge of her desk and avoided eye contact.

"Right, well, we have ourselves a little predicament here. But it doesn't need to be." Amber kept her voice low.

"It doesn't?" I asked, unable to keep my smirk hidden.

"We didn't know each other and were consenting adults last night. It was evident we both had a good time and personal details were unnecessary."

"Ah, you didn't want to know. And then you left, pretty much after your big orgasm."

She lifted her head. "Shh!"

"Well, you did a runner. Like I would usually, but you beat me to it. I can't say that's ever happened before." I adjusted myself in front of her.

"I haven't beat you to anything. Last night was just that. Last night. It will never happen again. I know I won't have any issue with that," she said, her voice unwavering, her body still.

Moving to the corner of her desk, I sat beside her, our thighs touching. "And you are so certain of that?"

She remained still. "Absolutely."

"Well, then, no more amazing sex."

She stood, giving me her back and turned to the nearby desk drawer to pull out a file. But it was too late, the blush on her neck had bloomed its way round to her nape.

"Please don't. There can't be any talk like that around here. It would jeopardize everything I've worked for…" she turned back around, "… your job might be nothing to you. But it's everything to me. I'm going to do my best for your brother, for this merger, and for you. Let's shake on it, forget it ever happened, and move on together, professionally."

She extended her hand which I took and held it in mine. Her stare steadfast.

She didn't give two shits about who I was. Amber cared more about her precious career than social climbing with an heir to a billion-dollar fortune. She was a woman with values. *Living proof they existed.*

"All right, deal. Let's hope we have separate rooms, for your sake."

She let out a nervous laugh, then cleared her throat.

"Please keep this between us. I don't want Chadwick or Carlton knowing and taking me off this case."

"Maybe."

"Maybe?" She straightened her posture with a perturbed look. "Now I know how it feels to be your brother."

A flush of blood filled my veins. "Careful." I turned my back, marching back down the hallway to the seventies elevator and back down to the waiting car where Josh, the chauffeur, stood out front. He opened the door, and I slid in the back seat, a familiar song playing throughout the car speakers.

"Smells Like Teen Spirit" by Nirvana, roared through the speakers. What better song to let off some steam than to a Kurt Cobain classic? "Hey Josh, turn it up," I said.

After a few more songs had passed, Carlton joined me in the custom, black-tinted SUV. You'd think we were rock stars with the amount of privacy and security my brother requested.

"What the hell was that?" Carlton's voice was coated in barbed wire.

"What? I behaved."

"Fuck me. I've just been apologizing to Chadwick about your sorry, lackluster ass…" he shook his head, "… at least you're in expert hands with Amber. She won't take any shit you throw her way. I could see it in her eyes."

Oh, brother, if you only knew. "You noticed that too."

He stared at me. "Don't you dare. Don't even think about it with her. Magma has a long-standing relationship with Chadwick Lane Lawyers, and I don't need you to come in here and fuck it all up with your dick. Tell me, is she going to be a problem for you?"

"Well, she is fucking gorgeous. Or are your balls in a vice so tight you can't see that?"

"All right, that's it." He reached into his jacket pocket and pulled out his phone.

"Hold up, what are you doing?"

"I'm calling Chadwick and asking him to assign someone else. Amber is out."

I flicked his arm away, sending the phone to the floor. "What the fuck are you talking about? I can control myself."

"Jesus, Logan." He picked up his phone from the carpeted floor mat. "Fine. Now turn this blaring music off, I have a conference call."

5

AMBER

"Excuse me, Miss Anderson, we'll be arriving at the airport in five minutes." Tom, my driver, smiled in the rearview mirror. He slowed, taking the highway exit.

"Thanks, Tom." Madeleine had arranged everything, and right on time, a black SUV arrived out front of my Seaview apartment. As per Madeleine's instructions, Logan and I were to meet at the Brisbane airstrip for our flight into Bundaberg. She was as efficient as she was obvious about sleeping with Logan. A flash of annoyance hit me. But not because they'd been together, but rather she was the type of girl to kneel before him because of his name. I shook away the judgment. *Was I any better?* I hadn't even caught Logan's name before sleeping with him.

An email caught my attention as I checked my phone. I thumbed out a quick reply, then slid it back into my briefcase's slip pocket. My gaze fell to the outside. The buildings warped into one, and the liquid amber trees rained confetti in the blustery breeze.

The last two days were a whirlwind. Seeing him in the boardroom left me unbalanced, like a yoga pose. I told myself I could ignore his smooth gray eyes, five o'clock shadow, and intimidating height. *I was sure I could.*

Regardless, my job came first. It had gotten me this far, and anything else was a distraction. And, come hell or high water, I had my rules. This trip would be fine. I'd just work night and day, avoiding the arrogant, shiny ornament of a man. Then, I'd be back to the safety of my matchbox apartment with my Netflix and research papers, like it didn't even happen. *Easy.*

I toyed with my necklace. The same one hadn't left my neck since the day I arrived in Seaview. The small, lion-face pendant, a find at the vintage shop and a daily reminder that building my resilience would ensure I never ended up like my mom. Not too long ago, I'd learned to shed the scars of my upbringing but not the guilt. It still ate away at me. And every phone call I'd put off making over the years stacked on the guilt like blocks in a Jenga Tower.

My phone pinged, pulling me out of the somber road my mind was traveling down. I pulled the device from my briefcase's slip pocket, and Jazzie's name flickered on the screen. *Damn it!* With everything going on, I'd completely forgotten to check in with her.

Jazzie: *Hey, I've arrived in NYC.*
I fired a text back. *Excellent. Good flight?*
Jazzie: *Turbulent. I wish I had your iron stomach.*
The car slowed, so I was all fingers and thumbs.
Amber: *Oh no! I'm on my way to the airport now. Wish me luck with the deal.*
Jazzie: *You'll nail it, like you always do. PS: Kit met me at the airport.* Heart emoji.

I smiled. I hoped whatever she had with one of the world's most popular rock stars was authentic. When he'd flown Lily and me over to New York a few months back, it had certainly seemed like the real deal.

It happened to be my first ever time on a plane and first-class at that. I'd insisted on paying for my economy airfare, but Kit just laughed at the offer, and I didn't bother pushing it, as much as it pained me.

I flipped out a quick reply.

Amber: *That's very sweet of him.*

Within a few seconds, my phone beeped with a message.

Jazzie: *Make sure it's not all work. Promise me you'll have some downtime?*

Amber: *Sure.*

I lied.

It was easier to lie to Jazzie and Lily the more work consumed me. Sixty-plus-hour work weeks were my norm, and they both half-joked one day they'd get a call from my boss saying he'd found me slumped over my desk with my fountain pen. They didn't hesitate when I asked them to be my emergency contacts. I didn't have anyone else.

They both thought I worked way too hard, and they were probably right, but what they labeled as obsessive was fast becoming my normal. I know they were only trying to look out for me, and maybe I should heed their advice. After all, they'd befriended me when they had zero reason to. We've been friends since school. Jazzie and Lily had reached out when they'd seen me eating lunch alone in the university grounds, and now, five years later, we're an inseparable trio. Well, mostly. Jazzie has found herself a rock star and moved to New York City, and Lily found her second chance at love with Blake.

Jazzie: *Hmm… miss you already.*

I quickly text back.

Amber: *Me too x*

This wasn't the time to focus on my personal life or that of my friends. I did a quick shake of my head as if it would help clear my thoughts and did my best to focus on the now.

The chauffeur pulled the car into a gateway and punched in a code. A few seconds later, the metal gates slid open. He drove onto the private strip, and a white and gold trim Cessna came into view.

Okay, so it was impressive.

Once again, I nestled my phone into my leather briefcase. In the duffle next to me, I'd packed blouses and skirts that looked the least worn and my favorite pair of thin-heeled stilettos. At the last minute, I'd thrown in some denim cut-off shorts, a casual tee, and a cotton dress. Even though it was autumn, the humidity in Queensland felt stickier than a candy apple.

Before I could lift the door handle to exit, the door opened from the outside.

"Allow me," Tom said as he reached into the back seat and retrieved my briefcase and duffle bag.

"Ah, thanks," I said, feeling awkward. Even if I were a gazillionaire, would I want someone to open doors and carry my bags? I wasn't without arms.

The whooshing sound of the jet pierced my ears, indicating Logan must be onboard already. I followed Tom toward the staircase leading into the jet.

As I entered, it was clear he wasn't around. "Where's Logan?" I asked, stepping into luxury.

"He should be here any moment," Tom said, placing both the briefcase and duffle bag down on one of the four seats.

"I checked my watch." We did have two minutes to spare, so he wasn't late, yet.

"Thank you, Miss Anderson. Have a splendid trip."

"Cheers, Tom." I took the seat next to my bags which left Logan one of the two remaining seats in front of me. At least this way, I could avoid him on the brief flight.

"Miss Anderson, welcome aboard. I'm James Grassy, your pilot today." A man in his early fifties, dressed in a double-breasted navy suit with four gold-striped epaulets on the shoulder and sleeve of his jacket, smiled.

"Lovely to meet you, James."

"It's only a short flight from here. I'm just waiting for Mr. Magma, and then we will be in the air."

"Thank you." He disappeared up ahead, and I nestled into the softest tan leather seats my body had ever had the privilege of melting into. And the most expensive, too, no doubt. I grabbed my laptop out of my briefcase, figuring I may as well get back to a few emails.

Time ticked by as I wrote email after email. I'd noticed a while ago, the pilot had shutoff something, so the whooshing sound of the propeller wasn't so loud, but the plane still *idled* if that was a thing.

Curious, I checked the time. Nine thirty. *So much for our nine o'clock departure.* My jaw tensed, and I threaded my necklace with my fingers.

"Finally." I heard the pilot mutter as he rose to greet Logan.

At his comment, I shifted my attention outside the cabin window. Strolling toward the plane, Logan appeared with mirrored aviator sunglasses and perfect, high fade hair.

Jesus, Maverick from Top Gun, *anyone?*

Wearing casual tan pants, a dress shirt, and Chelsea boots, he looked every bit the handsome heir to a fortune. I pushed the thought from my head as quickly as it came and the heat slashing my chest. If I was going to succeed on this trip—and I needed to—there would be no room for any lustful thoughts of him.

"Well, hello there. Should I kiss you or shake your hand?"

"Shaking my hand is perfectly fine." I extended my hand in his direction. "We were meant to leave half an hour ago."

"Oh, were we? Well, I'm here now." He walked down the aisle, brushing past my thigh, and my level of calm disappeared in a matter of seconds.

When I realized he was attempting to reach over me, to sit

where my bags were, I piped up, "Please leave my bags where they are," I said with a calm but firm tone.

"We should discuss this deal, Amber. Might be hard with my back in your face."

"Usually, when someone is running late, it's polite to let the other person know. We will now be late for the preliminary meeting with the CEO of Danker Gold."

"Relax. We'll get there."

Abruptly, I extended my arm, pressing my hand to my duffle bags as he was mid-lift.

"You seriously don't want me to sit here?" His expression told me he was shocked.

In response, I kept my hand firmly on my bag and gave him a pointed look.

"Mr. Magma, welcome. I'm your pilot, James Grassy. Can you please take your seat as we are ready for departure?"

"Sure thing, Jimmy." Logan said, turning back to face me. "I'll flip you for it."

"What? Are you seriously trying to play a childish game instead of taking a damn seat?"

I thought I would get a rise out of him, but his modelesque face didn't show one bit of a reaction. "Don't tell me you're scared you'll lose."

"Paleassse. Give me the damn coin."

A grin spread across his annoying face as he plonked the bag in its rightful position.

Cocky shit.

"Ladies first," he said, reaching into his pants pocket and pulling out a gold coin.

"Heads."

He smirked, his gunmetal eyes not missing a beat.

On reflex, I rolled my eyes in return and couldn't stop my head from the shake of disbelief. This was not how I envisioned today would go at all.

"Good, because tails never fails."

"Say's a betting man," I quipped.

"You better believe it, sweetheart." He tossed the coin into the air and caught it, slamming it down onto the back of his hand.

Anxious, I inched forward off my high-back chair as he slowly lifted his hand, exposing the coin.

"Looks like you're stuck with me." Logan grinned.

A low groan formed in my throat. How did I let myself get sucked into his childish little game?

Carelessly, he grabbed my bags, dropping them to the seat in front. The engine roared, and I was grateful for the noise.

"Mr. Magma, Ms. Anderson, welcome aboard the Sovereign Elite. We are ready for take-off."

Logan motioned a circular singular finger to the pilot. I guess that meant we were ready.

I wondered if private jets impressed him, or if they were as regular to him as hailing a cab. We taxied out to the runway and as I side-glanced Logan, I found him lost in thought. I ignored the curiosity creeping in.

Suddenly, we stopped, and the engine instantly roared to life. A second later, the jet shot forward like a slingshot, and my stomach lurched into my tonsils.

In only a few minutes, we were up high, cruising through endless cloudless blue skies.

"Hello, again. We can expect a cruising time of forty minutes into Bundaberg. Relax and enjoy the flight during this stunning day," the pilot's voice came through the intercom system.

I glanced over at Logan, who hadn't moved an inch, staring out the window like a drug. His body nonchalant like his entire demeanor.

Irritation coursed through my veins. Why on earth would

someone not care if they were late? What gives him the right to be late and make everyone else's day run behind?

We were nearly halfway into the flight, and he hadn't said a word. I should be thankful for the peace, but as each minute ticked by, my fidgeting worsened, and the more he ignored me, the more my skin burned.

Unable to take it anymore, I cleared my throat. Well, if he didn't want to be mature, I ought to. "Any suggestions on what we can say to the CEO of Danker Gold? By the time we get there, we'll be almost an hour late."

He ignored me, staring out the window like a patient on a horse tranquilizer. This only fueled my burning irritation.

"Hello?" I yelled.

He whipped his head around, his gaze leveling me. It took everything not to squirm as he stared at me.

"Well, you didn't answer me?"

"Does it matter? Let's just say I got caught up in traffic. I'm sure it happens all the time."

My cheeks puffed out as I let out an irritated breath. The man doesn't care, that much is obvious. I couldn't stop the resentment that took up residence on my face.

"People are late for meetings all the time, Amber." I ignored the way my name rolled off his tongue and pushed down the creeping blush.

"They are, but usually they are sorry about being late. Your lack of remorse is alarming," I mumbled.

"What was that?"

"Do you really want to know?"

"I wouldn't ask, Amber, if I didn't want to know."

Again, with the name. "I said, your lack of remorse is alarming, and FYI, I'm always early for a meeting. But they are my own set of values."

"Oh Jesus, Mother Teresa. It's just work."

"What would you know about work?" I asked.

Last night I'd googled all there was to know about Logan Magma. And I kind of wish I hadn't. I found out what I probably had already surmised from the boardroom. From dropping out of Cambridge to sailing yachts in the Caribbean, Greek Islands and Ibiza, Logan was the quintessential rich playboy. Attending society parties and splashing cash were as routine as brushing teeth.

"Ah. Nancy Drew is in the house. That's a change from the impulsive Amber in the alleyway. You know, I wish you hadn't researched me, that way you'd hold back your judgment before you truly knew me."

"Okay, for argument's sake, let's just say you're right. Maybe we should rewind a bit. Put a pause on the nit-picking… as hard as that might be."

"Is it unlike you to bite your tongue?" Logan pressed.

"You could say that."

"You don't seem like the ballsy girl who pulled me into the alleyway. In fact, you're like the coin we tossed a moment ago. One side is the impulsive, insatiable sexy girl that screams passion."

I blushed. *Dammit.*

"Then flip the coin over and here we are. Amber, controlled within an inch of her life, poised, leaving no room for error. No room for fun…" He paused, slowly casting his stare down my body. If I wasn't scarlet red before, I was now. He'd stripped me bare with his hooded eyes.

His gaze returned to mine. "I pick the girl in the alleyway."

"You're quite observant." I stared out of the cabin windows. Arid landscapes and dotted suburbs below came more into view as we started our descent.

"First time in a private jet?" Logan asked.

"Fiftieth time in a private jet?" A wry smile spread onto my red lips.

He shrugged. "Probably more."

"Have you ever thought about using the money for good?"

He exhaled, and a smirk formed on his face. "I guess you think I just spend money. I mean, it's what the papers report. And sure, I do. But you wouldn't understand. It would be nice, for once, with someone of your intellect, to realize that sometimes it's not exactly how the papers report."

Suddenly, there was a loud bang, and the plane jolted and swerved recklessly in the sky. My head slammed against the padded leather as I gripped the arm of the chair. A piercing alarm echoed through the cabin.

"Logan!" I yelled over the deafening alarm.

I grabbed my throbbing head, trying to shield it from thrashing about even more. The Cessna moved abrasively left to right, lower, then higher. My laptop crashed onto the floor as oxygen masks fell from the ceiling panel.

Oh my God—not like this—not now.

The pilot's voice came through the speakers, but I only made out every other word.

"Mayday... engine failure."

Logan stilled. It was as if he was frozen in his seat. "Logan," I yelled again.

This time, he whipped his head toward me. He must've seen the terror in my eyes because amidst the washing machine of turbulence, he reached for my hand and grasped it in his.

"Just breathe and brace yourself," he said calmly. "Continue to take even controlled breaths and put your head between your legs."

"I don't want to die like this," I yelled as I did what he told me to do and saw a trickle of blood from my head run down my knee. My breath grew shallow, my head lighter. He squeezed my hand tighter, and all I could focus on was how wrong this situation was. Right when everything was clicking together for me, this would be it? I didn't want to die now.

Hoping that this was some kind of mistake—a terrible nightmare—I squeezed his hand back.

After what felt like forever, the plane stopped jolting and thrashed about less. The loud banging stopped, and the alarm shut off.

I peered up from my knees, his hand unmoving.

The pilot's voice boomed. "Everyone okay?"

Logan stared at me, then back at the pilot. "We're fine. What the hell happened?"

"Left engine failure. I switched it off before the fire could take hold, but we are running on one engine. We will make it to Bundaberg on that. Landing in five minutes."

Logan talked to the pilot about the engine damage and fuselage. From their conversation, it sounded like he knew about planes. I closed my eyes and held onto his hand.

"Amber, it's okay. Everything is all right now."

With his other hand, he stroked my back. He leaned over and put his face as close as his seat belt would allow him. I absorbed his soothing touch and stared into his eyes, etched with—was that concern?

Confusion overwhelmed me, and I clutched my aching forehead. I let go of his hand and sat up straight, so his hand had no place on my mid-back.

"I'm okay," I lied.

6

LOGAN

By the time we touched down, we'd missed the scheduled meeting at Danker Gold with their CEO and a team of lawyers. So, I was late. Big fucking deal. With a quick phone call, I explained our near-death experience, and rescheduling for tomorrow was a cinch.

Irritated with the snail's pace the chauffeur was driving, I exhaled loudly. Distracting myself, I settled my gaze toward Amber. Her long black eyelashes fanned toward her thick eyebrows. Her appearance was fragile like a spider's web. She was anything but. If I got too close, she'd swallow me whole—just like the rest of them.

She'd remained silent since the engine failure, but the touch of her velvet hand gripping mine lingered. So did the fear in her eyes. When the piercing sound of the cabin alarm reverberated throughout my body and the plane tossed about like a beach ball held hostage to the breeze, I wanted to step up and be the man she needed me to be. She'd disarmed me with one look.

I was the guy with the black American Express card. Women saw me as their meal ticket, and I let them. Life was easier that way. But not today. No amount of money could buy myself out of a free-falling plane I found myself in with her.

My handful of flying lessons were useless with an engine out. Instead, I focused on what I could do—I rubbed her back while I held her hand, and it seemed to have slowed her panicked breathing. Then the pilot regained control, and the Cessna became less turbulent.

That's when she'd gone cold, distant, and withdrawn. Feelings I knew all too well.

But the strangest part of all was my own overwhelming feeling of sadness I'd had when the plane dropped. Sadness filled my ice-cold veins, not fear. In that moment, deep down, I knew no one had truly known me. No one would miss me. The opportunity to be known and understood had passed me by like a Mediterranean summer. If I'd died, no one would truly grieve.

"We're here," the chauffeur said, whipsawing me out of my spiral of self-pity.

The scenery outside my window caught my attention. Cabins rose out of the endless orange dirt road. In pairs, they stood with gray steel roofs and brick walls. Tiny homes, there must have been twenty of them, all identical and only differentiated by either a red or orange front door. "I think there must be some mistake."

The chauffeur checked his phone. "This is definitely the address I have. This is where the fly-in and fly-out engineers stay."

"Where are the cameras? I'm being punked." I laughed, but the driver only stared at me.

I twisted my head around, scouring the deserted stretch of terracotta earth for a hidden media pack. But all I did was strain my neck.

"Sorry, sir, were you expecting something different?"

"I'm sure he was," Amber muttered, picking up her briefcase.

"Look at this place, it's a dump! Where's the beach house?"

"Beach house? I don't know, maybe about two hours away! Anyway, it's not that bad, Logan," Amber said.

Was she serious?

I unlocked my phone and clicked on Madeleine's number. One ring later, she'd picked up. "Madeleine, what kind of shit accommodation is this?"

"I'm so sorry, Logan. The house I had turned out to be double booked."

"Well, un-book it!" I shouted.

"I can't do that." Her voice trembled, and instantly I regretted my tone. She didn't deserve the brunt of my frustration The last thing I wanted was to mimic my brother. We were nothing alike.

Once I was sure I was in control, I lowered my voice to a normal decibel. "Money fixes everything, Madeleine. Just double whatever they're getting." I stared at the metal matchbox building. "Actually, triple it."

Out of the corner of my eye, Amber's not-so-subtle shake of the head didn't go unnoticed. *I wasn't asking for a diamond-encrusted latrine. What's her problem?*

"I'm working on it, Logan, but you will have to stay there tonight. There are no vacancies nearby. Apparently, there's a fair this weekend so everything is booked solid."

"I couldn't care less if the Royals were in town, just get it sorted!" I snapped off the call. My calm demeanor leaving me once again.

"Oh, don't get your knickers in a knot. It's got the essentials. A bed, a roof, and most likely a kitchen." Her grin disappeared into a line.

Enjoyment poured out of her like rain. I wanted to hike up her knee-length skirt and plough into her like I hid in the alleyway. Just the thought swelled my dick against the cotton of my pants. "What am I going to do with a kitchen?"

Her hands jerked sharply, letting go of her bag and gestured her palms up to the roof of the car. "Cook. You know, food?"

A grunt escaped from the back of my throat. At this point, I wasn't sure what annoyed me more, her sass or the fact she'd rejected me. Flatly refusing to do what we did in Seaview again. I don't chase women. They do the chasing, but maybe I could charm her into working all day if we could slide between the sheets at night. Otherwise, hearing her smart mouth and not being able to touch her impossibly long legs and peach of an ass would be torture. More tortuous than the shoebox of a room that stood mockingly in front of me.

"Cabin three is for you, Mr. Magma, and four is for you, Ms. Anderson." The driver, in serious need of a shave, handed Amber her key, then handed me mine.

"There's enough space around here to have one of these to yourself, so what do they decide to do? Put two people under the one roof with a shitty dividing wall."

"Do you hear yourself?" Amber said, feeling her bandage. She'd stubbornly refused my help after I got her the first-aid kit, insisting on cleaning her head graze herself.

Maybe I came off brattish, but Jesus, the place was more deserted than summer break. I had a point. The land was vast, and we were at least an hour inland from the coast. It was just a waste to bunch up cabins in the outback.

I shrugged. "Look at this space. I could dance naked in the street and count the people on one hand that would bear witness."

She let out a laugh, impulsive and free. My skin hummed at the sound.

"Whatever you do, don't do that!"

I lowered my sunglasses, trailing my gaze over her body, then returning to her eyes. "Are you sure about that?"

Her eyes locked with mine, and for a moment we were back in the alleyway. She turned away first, fiddled with her lock, jamming the key left and right, trying to get it to click open.

"So, I'll see you tomorrow?" Before I could respond, she'd shut the door behind her.

The chauffeur returned with my bags, and I handed him a bill from my embossed Italian leather wallet. "Thanks, bud."

"Thank you, sir. I'm sorry this isn't what you thought, but perhaps you can find the beauty in these regions. They sure are on my bucket list."

"I doubt it, but thanks."

The inside of the cabin was blander than custard. There was smell—a weird combination of dirty socks and fresh paint invaded my nostrils.

I placed my Saint Laurent bowling bag on the rattan lounge inside the front door. They'd decorated—if you could call it that—the room with a timber coffee table, white round dinner table and chair, and a bed.

The only extravagance was the size of the main bed that greeted you a yard from the entranceway—king-size with a variety of pillows—at least it was long enough to accommodate my height. The leather headrest backed against the common wall, and if I guessed right and these cabins were a mirror image, the only thing separating us was a paper-thin wall.

A thud pulled me from the beige color of the floorboards and furniture melding into one. A flow of water echoed so I walked toward presumably the bathroom to see if I'd sprung a leak.

The faucet spurted with water, except it wasn't my faucet, but Amber's next door. I leaned against the square white wall tiles, their coolness tempering the backs of my arms. A few inches on the other side of the wall, Amber was showering, naked.

I peeled myself off the tiles. After all, I wasn't a creep. Walking toward the kitchen, I adjusted my swelling cock.

The kitchen spanned the length of my arm, with a two-burner hotplate and the smallest oven I'd ever laid eyes on. I opened the bar refrigerator underneath the counter, not expecting much, but the very thought of food made my stomach rumble.

Surprisingly it was full. I fished about, finding a block of cheese, a bottle of wine, some red meat covered in plastic wrap, milk, and a few other wrapped packages. At this late stage, if I wanted to eat something, then I'd need to find it here and cook it myself. I swiped my hand through my brow. *Fuck me.* I don't ever remember having to cook myself a meal.

The bottle of red stood tall. It would do. I reefed out a budget wine glass, then another, trying to locate one not cloaked in a film of dust.

I flicked a text to my brother. This situation had Carlton's name written all over it.

Logan: *Is this some sick joke you and Dad are playing at?*

After I poured my glass, I sipped my wine. It was rancid, but I punished myself by drinking more. Finally, my phone beeped.

Carlton: *I don't have a clue what you're talking about.*

Yeah, I'm calling bullshit on that one. I bet he signed off this accommodation from the start. Seeing if his baby bro could rough it. Well, screw him.

Logan: *Sure, you don't. Do you know the plane lost power?*

Immediately my phone pinged.

Carlton: *I heard about that.*

Well, fuck you! I threw my phone, and it hit the wall. It wasn't like I needed confirmation I wasn't worthy of their love, but he sure as hell spelled it out then with his lack of care and worry.

I took another swig and topped off my glass. In a matter of minutes, I'd emptied half a bottle. Well, too bad if I missed some little detail yet vital component of their precious deal—they'd just have to deal with it.

* * *

A tapping at the door woke me. I opened my eyes, and the lightness of the cabin had faded. *How long had I been sleeping?*

Another knock sounded, but this time louder. "Logan?"

Hearing Amber's voice, I jolted as it cut through the hollow door.

"Coming," I said, somewhat unsteadily on my feet as I walked the two steps to the front door.

I swung it open, and the damn thing nearly swung off its hinge.

"Hi," she said.

Wearing denim jeans and a tee-shirt, she resembled the girl from the restaurant a few days ago rather than the polished control colleague I'd since been accustomed to.

"Hi, straight back at you." I grinned. Maybe we could be fuckbuddies after all.

She peered past me as her gaze fell onto the bottle on the table and the empty glass.

"I thought as much."

She pushed past me. "I'm making you dinner."

"Er, why?"

"Because I know you probably don't know how. And I need you sharp tomorrow."

"Oh, so this is all for your benefit, then, is it?"

"I can leave?" she questioned tersely.

I shook my head. "Don't," I said, and our eyes met like they did in the alleyway.

She was the first to break the iron-clad stare we shared. You'd have to be on Pluto to miss that chemistry. She shimmied straight past me. I closed the door to the dingey cabin and flicked the light on. It flickered like a strobe light at a party, and I laughed. "Wow, we really are living large, aren't we?"

With her head in the refrigerator, my focus rested on her perfectly round ass.

She swung her head around, clasping one hand on the bar refrigerator. "Don't be a snob. It's just a light bulb that needs changing."

"Well, you'd think they do that before checking someone in?"

She rolled her large hazel eyes at me as she stood with a few handfuls of a variety of food from the refrigerator.

"Okay, steak and salad are what's on the menu."

"Is it Wagyu?" I asked.

"Where is the frying pan?"

"You're asking me?"

"Well, find it because I want to play ping pong with your head. Is it Wagyu?" She shook her head, and a slight grin split into her cheeks.

I flopped on the lounge and watched her work the kitchen like it was her own—chopping tomatoes, washing lettuce, and cooking something on the stove which seriously was making my mouth salivate. I wondered what her own place looked like. She seemed to loath my wealth, so perhaps she didn't live in the best quarters, after all.

"So, why law?"

She shrugged with her back to me, giving me the perfect excuse to zero in on her ass again.

"I'm anal about research, extremely analytical, and very meticulous."

I snorted a laugh.

"What?" She looked at me with a side eye. But hell would freeze over before I told her it was her choice of words and me zeroing in on her ass.

"Nothing, go on."

"It was one of the highest-paying jobs straight out of college."

"Did you actually research what the highest-paying jobs were before you chose a degree?"

"Of course," she said, immediately.

At my silence, she turned toward me with a cleaver in her hand, her brows knitted together. Immediately, I put my hands up in surrender.

With an exhausted sigh, she set the knife down. A look of exasperation overcame her beautiful face. "You wouldn't understand why anyone would look at remuneration over career choice, I guess."

"No. Money to me was always there, flowing like Niagara Falls. They had given me everything." *And nothing. Nothing of actual value anyway.*

"Sounds like the perfect upbringing."

Sure. If you categorized emotional detachment as perfect.

"Wasn't it?" she asked, peeling me away from spiraling thoughts.

"Oh yeah, it was fabulous." I couldn't hide the sarcasm dripping from my words.

She narrowed her eyes.

"Well, if you count being shipping off overseas at the age of thirteen to do your schooling, fab, it could have been had the reason not being for the sole purposes of a better education. Instead, they shipped me off because I was a nuisance to the family."

Her face fell, and the last thing I wanted from her, or anyone, was pity. I didn't deserve that. After all, I was born into privilege with money, nannies, and the best education. Why would anyone pity me?

"How's that steak coming along? I could eat the ass out of a donkey."

She whipped her head around and pursed her lips. "If you're not careful, you can get it yourself."

I stood up quietly and stepped behind her. Her warmth emanated from her glowing skin. I didn't touch her but standing only inches away had awakened something inside of me.

I lowered my face to her ear, "Maybe I will."

She froze. Our bodies so close, I could feel her warmth—her scent, tantalizing and fragrant like soapy linen and gardenias.

She tilted her head, so her lips were inches from mine, then cleared her throat.

Taking a step toward the hotplate, she grazed my chest. She arranged the steak in the frying pan, and it sizzled and popped.

I stepped back and exhaled, not trusting myself to remain this close to her.

With her back still to me, she hovered around the frying pan. A blush appeared between her shoulders below her neck as silence descended inside the cabin.

Salty and caramelized flavors filled the room, the extraction of the rangehood not powerful enough to remove the thin veil of smoke in the air.

"I guess we'll have these here?" She tilted her head toward the round table in the corner.

"Sure." I stepped toward the table, grazing her thumb as I grabbed my plate. "Smells amazing." I said, staring at her.

She sat down, clearing her throat. "Logan, I have rules." Her voice was even, but her cheeks glowed bright.

My knife met no resistance when I sliced it into the steak like It was cutting butter. "Rules?"

"Yes, rules."

"Well, are you going to leave me in suspense?" I popped the steak into my mouth, and although it wasn't Wagyu, it was cooked perfectly rare and hit the spot.

"Rule one. Never sleep with the same man twice. Rule two. Never mix business with pleasure."

She hadn't started eating but sat opposite, assessing me, waiting for my reaction.

I laughed. But when her expression remained the same dead-serious look, I realized she wasn't joking.

"You're serious?"

"As a rattlesnake."

"Why?"

"Because." I wanted to press but figured now was not the time. We had time to pick this up again.

"Well, that's a damn shame."

She shrugged, clutching her thin metal fork as she pierced a perfectly quartered tomato.

"We could have really had fun here together…"

"No."

"I know it wasn't just me who felt that insane connection in the alleyway in Seaview."

She coughed as though the tomato had lodged in her throat. "So about tomorrow… we're meeting the head of Danker Gold and Wendy from legal. They will give us a rundown of the mine. Also, the accounting firm you hired will be there. They are flying in tomorrow so we can all meet and work together on reviewing the equipment and looking into the mining leaseholds."

Her lawyer exterior was back, and I exhaled.

"Great."

She dropped the cutlery, and it clattered on the table. "That's all you can say? Great?"

"Well, to me, it's not as exciting as it is for you." Not wanting to continue the conversation, I tore into my steak like I couldn't get enough it—piece after piece, I wolfed it down, my mouth too busy to speak. After I'd finished, I glanced up to see her staring at me.

"If it stacks up, and your company gains Danker Gold, then it certainly adds a few extra zeros to your bank account."

"I don't care about that."

"Sure, you do," she said, then resumed eating.

I grinned. "The yachts are nice. This time last year, the Mediterranean was my playground. Island hopping in Sardinia and Corsica and drinking thirty-year-old scotch as though it were water."

"You really aren't helping me like you right now."

"Have you ever been?" I asked, purposefully ignoring her statement.

"To Italy, no."

"You're missing out. The food, the people, the love, and passion…"

"I went to New York recently, and that's the extent of my overseas holidays."

"But you're what, early twenties? How is that the only place you've visited?"

Her gaze fell to the floor.

"Sorry, I don't mean to pry."

"Yes, you do. I work, that's why. I don't have a trust fund. It's just me in this equation, and I work damn hard to keep it that way."

"Well, all right."

"We couldn't be more opposite, could we?"

I imagined walking alongside her on the footpaths beside the canals in Venice and quickly shook away the thought. She was right, we couldn't be more opposite. "Maybe one day you'll go."

"I know I will." She lifted her gaze to mine, and we stared at one another. The air between us heated and crackled.

"Might be on your own, though, if you don't break one of those insane rules of yours."

She tilted her head and glared at me. "Well, at least it's on my dime."

"Touché, Amber. Touché."

She twisted her lips, then released them into a smile.

"I'm surprised you didn't recognize me in Seaview."

"I didn't realize you shared the same level of fame as George Clooney." She cocked an eyebrow.

"Hardly, but I frequently appear in the society pages here and overseas."

She lifted her head back, "And, am I meant to be impressed by that?"

"You, impressed? No. A lot of women make a beeline for me because of my family name and—"

"Well, lucky you," she interrupted before I even had a chance to finish.

I sighed. This wasn't coming out how I'd intended. "What I'm trying to say, if you let me, is you saw me as a guy in the bar and not a Magma man."

"Well, had I known you, I would have strayed like a cat." She folded her arms across her chest.

I leaned forward, my torso cut against the curve of the table. "That would be a first."

"Am I meant to pity you for all the casual sex you've notched up from gold-diggers?"

I regarded her. "I don't want your pity, Amber." Or anyone else's.

I ate the rest of my meal, but as delicious as it tasted, my appetite waned.

7

AMBER

Ugh. He was so frustrating! Like a leech drawing blood, Logan was getting under my skin. And I was letting him like the sucker I apparently am.

Last night, I tossed and turned when I should've been resting for the big few days ahead. Thoughts of him plagued me. Dinner was equal parts frustrating and interesting. When he'd let slip they shipped him off at a young age abroad to do his schooling, I noticed, if only for a second, a sadness lurking behind his eyes.

More than once, I was frustrated when his piercing gray eyes and angular jaw had caught me off guard. He could shoot pools of heat into my belly without so much as laying a finger on me. Logan's mere proximity was more than enough. Deep down, I knew better. His steely good looks masked the man who lay underneath. A rich playboy without a care for anyone but himself. He lacked what I had in spades— values and work ethic. I could never be with anyone like that.

He mocked my rules, but perhaps he was the one who should have rules or goals. Anything but the lofty concept of life he'd adopted and his ability to simply float through it. From the slither in the curtain, the morning sun cast a shadow on the wall.

Exhausted, from a sleepless night, I threw everything back into my briefcase. Up before dawn, I'd already sunk my teeth into perusing the asset sheet the accountants would review over the next few days. From haulage and excavation to geotechnical, explosive, and drilling equipment, everything was included in the Magma purchase. I'd been privy to that. Chadwick ensured we all were a team and operating as one, rather than the accountants doing one job and I another.

Yet, even as I zipped up my briefcase, I wondered if the inkling to his childhood wasn't as peachy and privileged as I'd prejudged.

Curiosity consumed me as I sat on the edge of the bed. Maybe the masked man was a facade to forget his own heartache and not the other way round. *Then why couldn't that be said of me too?* I wrapped all my value on work and crazy hours around building my success. Setting up rules to ensure I'd never end up back to the place full of abuse and fear, the place I swore I'd never return to, ever. *No, that was different.*

With a force I didn't realize, I roughly ran the brush through my shoulder-length hair, causing me to flinch at the harsh treatment. I exhaled. Again, this time slowly, I lifted the brush and combed it through my knotted tresses.

This wasn't the time or place to have my head in the clouds. I needed to focus on the here and now. Today, I'd be meeting my counterparts of the merger team. Chadwick had given me this amazing opportunity, and there was no way I was going to let Logan ruin it. Frustrated with myself, I let out an unfamiliar sound from the back of my throat, expressing my irritation.

Staring into the floor-length mirror facing the foot of the king-size bed, I pulled my hair back into a ponytail. After plaiting it, I wound it around the elastic into a neat bun. I tucked a few stray hairs into place and reassessed, but all I could see was his face on mine. The tingling sensation that shot up my spine every time he smiled in my direction, tempting me to bend and stretch my own rules, threatened to consume me.

"No." I yelled toward the mirror. The outburst surprised me. I'd do everything I could not to let Chadwick down.

Hoping to shake his presence off me, I shook my head. *Focus on the day, Amber.* The red digits on my side-table clock glared. In under ten minutes, the car would be out front. As I grabbed my things, I realized I hadn't heard a peep from Logan. Even if he was as quiet as a mouse, the paper-thin walls would have amplified some kind of movement.

He might already be ready, but I highly doubted that.

Quickly, I double and triple-checked my briefcase, making sure nothing had been left out, then walked out the door.

A combination of worry and dread descended over me as I tapped on Logan's door. I strained to hear movement on the other side, but I was met with a deafening silence.

Now clearly agitated, I proceeded to tap on his door with a heavy hand while I said, "Logan, you ready?"

Frustration mounted with each second ticking by and still, nothing.

My tapping turned to knocking before I pounded on his door. When there was still no response, I twisted the doorknob, and to my surprise, it was unlocked. I opened it and stepped inside.

I gasped at his sleeping form. "Logan!" The sheer force of my voice would have woken the dead.

He jerked his head off the pillow, the sheet sliding off him, revealing deliciously defined stomach muscles and a line of dark hair from his navel down to his exposed white briefs. Oh, and his morning wood, thick and glorious bulged through his briefs.

To ignore the heat pooling between my legs, I turned away.

"What time is it?" His voice was laced with guilt.

"Time to go! The driver will be here in five minutes, and you're in your goddamn underwear!"

"Care to break one of your rules?"

I spun on my stilettos. Shock coursed through my veins. "Go. Get up, shower!"

He grinned, a schoolboy grin that sent my fists into balls by my sides.

"I'm so angry right now!"

"You sure about that?" he said, pushing me to boiling point, and by the look on his face, he was pretty pleased with himself.

"Logan. *Now!*" This time my yell was so loud, I didn't recognize myself.

"All right! All right!" He shot out of bed, flinging the sheet off him.

Fuck! As I watched his back muscles tense from the movement, I tried to contain my emotions from boiling over. I took a sharp intake of breath when my gaze traveled over his broad shoulders, down to the seducing V-shape at his waist, and long carved legs glided like a well-oiled machine.

The shower sputtered, and I heard him groan. "Ah, *fuck!*"

I giggled, ignoring the confusing blend of irritation and attraction coursing through me. I knew the temperamental nature of the shower when earlier I, too, had a whoosh of cold water cut through the steaming heat. *Take that!*

Knowing it was best, I waited outside the cabin on the patio chair. Rules can't be broken that way. He'd left the bathroom door slightly ajar, probably accidentally, but the thought of curving my neck around to get a better view wasn't a good idea. Temptation was a powerful thing. And I'd only be lying to myself if I said the sight of him didn't tempt me. Then there was the fact he was a walking, talking orgasm.

Of all the men I'd slept with, Logan was the only one to

tempt me to come back for more. My rules that kept me safe were questionable when I was around him. Not just one, but both. I cursed myself for just thinking about it. This trip would be the death of me.

The driver pulled up in a black SUV, and I checked my watch. There was no way I'd allow us to be late today. If it came to it, I'd leave without him.

"Morning, Ms. Anderson. I'm Christopher, your driver while you're here in town." Formalities never sat well with me, especially since Christopher also appeared in his early twenties.

"Hi, Christopher, call me Amber. Logan isn't far behind." At least I silently hoped. I got up from the cane chair outside of my cabin door, smoothing down my black pencil skirt.

"Sure, let me, Amber," he said, offering to take my briefcase.

"It's fine, I've got it, thanks." He opened the door to the back door to the SUV, and I slid in. The seats were a buttery cream leather which made it easy to sit as I continued to wait for Logan. At least I was comfortable.

Almost five minutes ticked by as I oscillated between checking my wristwatch and my emails. My throat bobbed up and down as I swallowed down the rising exasperation. Technically, Logan and Magma were clients of Chadwick Lane Lawyers, but that wouldn't stop me from telling him exactly what was on my mind. I had our tryst to thank for that.

My ears pricked at the sound of a door slamming. He dashed toward the SUV. Dressed in a tailored gray suit and crisp white shirt, he'd turned his wayward billowy hair into a neat and, dare I say, professional style. I envied how quickly and effortlessly he'd showered and changed, looking every bit the walking temptation he was.

"Morning," he said like a pesky child at the foot of the bed and not the man with a multi-million-dollar merger on his mind.

"Hi." His subtle sandalwood cologne, the same one I remembered from the alleyway, filled the SUV.

"Ready to go, Mr. Magma?" Christopher looked from Logan to me in the rearview mirror.

"Yes," we both said at the same time.

After a few minutes, we pulled into a large parking lot and stopped. I opened the door before Christopher could get to it. To the right of the parking lot stood the unmistakable one-and-a-half-mile wide, open-cut gold mine. A feat in sheer enormity and scale, the mine was nestled inside the surrounding native forests. The mine couldn't be more out of place than a nun at a Guns N' Roses concert.

"First time at a mine?" Logan grinned.

"You can do better than that, Mr. Magma, surely?" I said over the heavy sound of machinery.

"I'd like to haul you out of here, then drill my—"

"Logan!" I frantically cast my eyes around. Thankfully, Chris had taken a call, and no one else was within earshot.

"You asked for it," he said, looking mighty pleased with himself.

I ignored the tingling feeling which began to rise in my belly and smoothed my hair back toward my bun. I didn't have time for foreplay. We had ten minutes to converse with the accountants appointed for the transaction before our rescheduled meeting with the team from Danker Gold. I'd allowed for that time. Ten minutes was just enough—t would've been fifteen if Logan hadn't slept in.

"Right, this way, please," Chris said.

Immediately, I walked ahead of Logan, keeping step with our driver. The thin needle of my stiletto black pumps seemed so out of place in the harsh landscape, but I didn't care. I also didn't care if they lifted me a few extra inches, making my already tall stature taller than your average male. Maybe it was the extra shot of confidence my height gave me in a male dominated industry. But not with Logan. His muscular frame still towered over me.

In the distance appeared dozens of portable buildings stacked high like Lego pieces forming a U-shape. Workers came and went from their accommodation to the mine at all hours. Fluorescent items of clothing flung haphazardly across the makeshift verandas and soccer nets at each end of the building hinted toward some after-hours fun.

"Here we are. Here's my card, Mr. Magma. Call me when you'd like to go back home." Logan took Chris's card and slid it inside his suit pocket.

"Now?" Logan asked.

I cast a frown at Logan and noticed in my periphery, Chris pause.

"He's joking," I said and waved to Chris. He smiled before walking back to the parking lot.

I headed toward the entrance noticing Logan walking alongside me.

"I wasn't, actually."

Standing at the entry to the largest portable white building, two men in suits were walking toward us.

"Too late now," I said under my breath.

"You must be Logan." The shorter, rounder, and balding man extended his hand. "I'm Vincent from Lloyds chartered accountants, and this is my associate, Jacob."

Logan shook their hands, then turned toward me, "And this is Amber Anderson, our head of legal from Chadwick Lane Lawyers."

Vincent cast his stare over me, his eyebrows melded into one. "Surely not?"

"Sorry?" I asked. A jab of irritation pricked my temples. *Did he really just glare at me from top to bottom?*

"No disrespect, Amber, but you look barely out of law

school," he sneered as his associate, Jacob, let out a barely audible laugh, then he turned his glare toward Logan.

"Vincent, Amber is—"

I held my hand up to cut Logan off. I didn't need anyone fighting my battles for me. Working in a male-dominated industry meant it wasn't my first time I'd come up against a sexist jerk, and I knew Vincent could trample me if I didn't stamp it out now.

"No disrespect, Vincent, but if we went by appearances, one could presume at any moment a myocardial infarction could take out our lead accountant, leaving us in an unfathomable predicament."

Logan let out an audible laugh, but my steely gaze remained on the dimwit of a man in front of me. He blinked feverishly and turned on his heel, leaving Jacob to scurry behind him.

As soon as I was sure they weren't going to turn back, I released my white-knuckled fingers from the tight ball behind my back.

"Damn, Amber." Logan stared with curiosity behind his grays.

"Too much?" I said, trying to regain a normal breathing pattern.

"That was fucking sexy."

Laughter spilled from my lips, and my pent-up tension eased. As we walked inside the building, Logan's hand grazed mine. I sucked in a breath, ignoring the rush it gave me.

So much for having time with Vincent and Jacob before the meeting. As we came up behind them, they turned, and Vincent leaned in saying something to Jacob as they sat in the only two seats in the foyer. Glued to their phones, they clearly weren't interested in engaging further.

"Mr. Magma and guests, please come through." The receptionist, blonde and petite, held her heated gaze longer than necessary on Logan.

Logan turned to me, ignoring the busty woman. "Showtime."

"Why don't we let Amber run with this, Vincent?" Logan said, slapping the middle-aged man between the shoulder blades.

What? A blush crept up my neck. Vincent let out a muffled groan obviously displeased with Logan's suggestion. The door opened to the boardroom, and two men in ill-fitting suits walked toward us. One suit barely done up, pulled at the button, whereas the other one almost dripped off him. Clearly this wasn't their usual attire.

Logan outstretched his hand as they approached. "Hello. Logan Magma."

"Yes, of course, I recognize you. Taylor Reed, Operations Manager, and this is our General Manager, Burt Kenson."

He shook both men's hands, then turned to me. "Meet our onsite acquisition team, Amber Anderson, Vincent Wiltshire, and Jacob Cho."

Taylor commanded attention and moved to greet the rest of us. I had to stand my ground and let it be known I belonged in this business. There was no way I was going to let a repeat of my earlier exchange with Vincent.

"That's a nice grip you got there, Amber," Taylor said.

"That she does." Logan grinned an impossibly wide smile. I fired him bullets with my eyes but held the polished professional smile I'd rehearsed many times before. Vincent sideways glanced, imparting a subtle glare, but one that didn't go unnoticed.

Over the next few minutes, we shook hands and exchanged the normal pleasantries.

Before any more time was wasted, I interrupted, "Shall we?"

"Please," Logan said, signaling for me to lead the way. I stepped past him, close enough for his woody scent to ignite my senses while feeling the weight of his heady stare.

Jesus, not now, Amber!

Inside the simple makeshift boardroom, I noticed another woman as we took our seats. I set about arranging my documents, laptop, and stationery on the table. I couldn't help but glance in her direction as I placed everything.

"I'd like you to meet Leila, she'll be your go-to person around the mine," Taylor said.

"Nice to meet you, Leila. I'm Amber Anderson." I smiled at the girl with purple pixie hair and fire-truck red lipstick who seemed by her genuine smile, abundantly happy to be in the presence of another female who wasn't the lone receptionist.

"Leila will run you through the OHS, and you'll each get a hardhat and visor, which you must wear when you step outside these offices," Taylor said.

"We don't want you getting lost or getting squashed by a CAT truck," Burt added. "That's PR we can't afford." Burt's stare fixed on Logan.

Logan's body shifted from relaxed to rigid.

What an asshole! I gripped my seat. I didn't like the dig Burt fired his way, but I was powerless to do anything about it.

"I expect you'll be here only four days conducting your due diligence?" Burt continued.

"I think that should work. However, if we need more time, is that an issue?" I asked.

"I think four days will be plenty," Vincent piped up, his smile hiding the spite in his eyes. *God, getting him to dislike me in a matter of minutes wasn't my intention.*

"If you need it for the deal to get across the line, then so be it," Taylor said.

"I couldn't imagine Logan staying in a deserted place like this for longer than four days. Must be just a tad different from the countless parties and opportunities in Europe." Burt's mottled face wrinkled, his smile turning upward into his hollow cheeks.

Inappropriate much?

"A slight change, but I'm making do." He tapped his fingers on the armchair repeatedly, his gaze regarding the General Manager.

Did they know one another, or was I the only one who hadn't read page six?

"We've received the auditing list. I don't think I need anything else from you, Taylor, except the inspections," Vincent said.

"Leila will help you with that." Taylor tilted his head in her direction.

Shifting focus back to me, I cleared my throat. "So shall I speak to you, Taylor and Burt, about the leases and compliance, or would Leila be privy to that?"

Burt directed his gaze toward me. "You can speak to me, in my office. I'm sure Taylor has another meeting to get to."

Leila glanced at me and held it pointedly. I read something behind her eyes only another woman could understand and tilted my head toward Logan. His nostril flared, but he held his attention on Burt who was still waiting for my reply.

I cleared my throat about to speak until Logan shifted.

"Great, I'll join you both. In your office, is that right, Burt?" Logan fixed his gaze on Burt.

Burt wrapped his fingers along the table in a stare-off with Logan, which made me uncomfortable. "Fine. Well, if we're done here, Leila, Vincent, and Jacob can head out to start the audit trail, and we can begin. We can stay here, instead."

"Great," Logan beamed. I turned toward Logan as the others motioned toward the door. His eyes held mine for a moment longer than plausible, an unreserved kindness shown to me.

"Is there any good coffee around here?" Logan broke the moment. "This tastes like dirty dishwater."

Taylor and Burt looked at one another, and I lowered my head into my folder trying to stifle a grin.

"I'll see what we can arrange for you," Leila offered as she led the accountants away, leaving Burt, Logan, and me in the enormous boardroom.

"Vincent is right, four days is a long time to be in the middle of nowhere. I'm sure we can wrap this up sooner than that, then I can be on my way."

I glared at Logan. We didn't know asset A from B, let alone the statutory approvals and compliance details. Too many unknowns could railroad the timeline completely.

I shuffled my papers in front of me. "What I'm sure Logan meant to say was, we will do our utmost to make it a quick and seamless process, but we will endeavor to investigate every item on the Heads of Agreement." I stared at Logan.

"What the lady says," Logan said sarcastically.

Taylor stood and excused himself from the boardroom, leaving Logan and me with Burt. Just as I was about to speak, Burt's phone rang, interrupting me. Without so much as a word, he held his index finger up at me and took the call.

"What was that?" I said in a low voice. "Can you at least try to pretend you want to be here? I'm trying my best to do this for your company. The least you could do is appear interested."

"I could think of a million other places where I'd much rather be than here. This office smells like stale farts and old feet."

"Well, go. What's stopping you? You don't have to be here. Just go."

"Unfortunately, I have to be here."

Before I could question him further, Taylor walked back in. "I'm going to leave you here with Burt. I've got to get to another meeting, so I'll catch up with you all later. If you need anything, contact either of us, and we will do our best to accommodate you."

"Thank you," I said.

"If you have time, Amber, I'd suggest you explore some wonders in the region," Taylor added.

"I bet there are some *real* wonders," Logan said, sarcastically.

Two hours had passed as I diligently went through the list of questions I'd prepared earlier. I'd got a lot of information and directions to begin my lines of inquiry relating to government leases.

Logan yawned next to me, not even trying to cover his mouth with his hands. I couldn't stop my irritated reaction that followed.

"Are we boring you, Logan?" Burt asked.

"No, no," Logan said. "Actually, let's be honest… a bit."

"Logan," I said, and Burt looked from me to Logan, then back again to me.

"I bet he is tough to tame."

"He's not mine to tame," I said, feeling the blush creep up from my toes to my torso.

"Actually, she's the tough one," Logan said.

"Well, if that's that, Amber, I think I've given you everything and more than you asked of me. I share your passion to find out everything you need to get the deal done. And we are an open book." Burt thankfully diverted the conversation.

"Excellent. Well, if I have any follow-up questions, I know who to ask." I sincerely hoped Burt didn't suspect something going on between Logan and me. That was the last thing I needed.

"I'll leave you to it. Leila organized a lunch platter for you both." He flicked his wrist toward his silver watch. "Although, its past lunch now. You're welcome to stay here in the boardroom or you can take the picnic to the viewing platform, which has a stunning aerial view of the landscape."

"The boardroom is fine," I said, trying to dissuade any romantic notions Burt may have of Logan and me. Plus, the idea of a picnic sounded slightly unprofessional.

"Don't be such a drag, we've been sitting here for hours. I need to stretch my legs. We'll take lunch outside," Logan said.

Annoyance coursed through me. And as he flashed his perfect smile, I relinquished. "So be it."

"Excellent, I'll arrange for a cart to take you up," Burt said.

8

LOGAN

On the viewing platform where we sat, the view was remarkable. Far from a romantic picnic, we were staring into an open dry pit that stretched football fields wide and deep. The landscape, vast and arid but still awe-inspiring in its own right. It wasn't Monte Carlo with lush emerald-green hills set against the turquoise waters, but here, sitting on a criss-crossed Scottish-looking picnic blanket opposite a laid back, hungry Amber, I strangely didn't want to be anywhere else.

"I'm starved," Amber said, removing her jacket. The breeze pressed against her cream blouse and teased me with of the outline of her lilac lace bra.

Suddenly, my mind was back there. In the alleyway. The soapy scent of her chestnut hair before the rain drenched it. Her natural full breast in my mouth, sucking and feeling her nipple swell with my touch. *Shit. Think excavators, haulers, due diligence. Anything else.* My engorgement pressed against the fabric of my pants, and I shifted awkwardly on the picnic blanket, subtly trying to adjust myself.

Opening up the flip-top lid to the cane basket that

reminded me of something from the Jane Austen period, I lifted out two glass containers with rubber lids. "Dare I ask what's in these?" I said, focusing on anything but her lace bra.

"Surely, only the finest for you, Mr. Magma," she said, her gaze set on mine. She was mocking me or flirting. I couldn't tell which.

She took the containers from my hand and lifted the lids. "Well, sorry to disappoint you, but it's not caviar."

"Pfft! I couldn't possibly eat it then." I grinned, enjoying this side of her.

"Good. I can have both Baguettes then."

"I bet you would just to prove a point."

She ran her teeth over her lips, then took an excruciating bite. The very satisfied face she made was one I'd seen before. *I watched her as her head flung back, and I entered her again in the alleyway, giving her what she needed, watching the ecstasy on her face.*

"All right! Baguette me!" I relinquished, reaching for the crusty bread with overflowing meats, cheese, and pickles.

Actually, it wasn't half bad. I followed her gaze as it set over the vast hole in the earth. Her flawless olive skin almost appeared iridescent under the afternoon sun. Her hair, pulled back in a neat bun showed streaks of lighter browns and auburns under the light. She was a complete contradiction to the dry scenery, and I welcomed it.

"What are you staring at?" she asked, her voice soft as she wiped away the imaginary food from her mouth.

"You, eating. You're hungry." I tried to deflect the gawking. She'd make light of me staring at her pink lips or the coral blush on her cheeks.

She put down the baguette. God knows why, she only had a bite left in it.

"Don't do that on my account. I'm rather enjoying watching you masticate that food in your mouth."

She burst out laughing. Then, as if surprised at her own involuntary response, she placed a hand over her mouth.

As she wiped the crumbs off her skirt, she asked, "So, how do you think it went in there?"

"I have my thoughts, but what do you think?"

She exhaled. "Can I be honest?"

"I wouldn't expect anything but honesty from your lips." I diverted my gaze to her full lips, thinking about her insatiable need for me in the alleyway. The way we'd connected was like moths to a lamp, devouring one another under the teeming night sky.

"I think you still don't give a damn about this merger…"

Her honesty dragged me away from my fantasy carousel. I rubbed my forehead.

"Not what you were expecting?" she asked.

"I'm invested," I said. Truth was, I watched her in the boardroom commanding the veterans like she, too, was in the game of M and A for forty years rather than a rookie.

"That's you trying? I'm confused why you are here rather than partying in Ibiza or yachting wherever it is you rich people yacht."

"Rich people?"

"Well, there's no point sugar-coating it."

I ran a hand through my hair, the wind ruthless up here.

"My brother and father dragged me back to Perth, after all this time, because they thought I needed to be tamed."

"Well, from what the tabloids say, they are probably right."

I tilted my head. "Haven't I said not everything is true."

She mimicked my head movement and tilted hers. "But mostly?"

"I'm the one they sent overseas. The one they wanted far, far away from their precious life. They were too quick to cast me away."

She squinted, gazing at me with curiosity. What was that expression?

"Yes, they sent me away to boarding school and cut all ties with me after I set fire to the east wing of the house at age twelve."

"Why did you do that?"

"I don't know." *I needed a cry for attention.*

"Do you think they loved your brother more than you?"

I twisted my lips. "What happened to never mixing business with pleasure?"

"That's purely a sexual thing."

"Thanks for the clarification."

"But look, it's okay, I get it. I don't enjoy talking about private stuff either," she said.

I took another bite of my baguette and stared out over the mine.

"It was always about my brother. Everything from when we were kids… he would always have one-on-one time with Dad… he'd get the extra tutoring, the accolades. I'd always be the first one they'd blame, even when most of the time it wasn't my fault. Then they'd decided I wasn't good enough for the family name and sent me to England to a strict boarding school. Each year, more to save face than actually want me back, I'd fly back for Christmas, but really by then, it was like I wasn't a part of the family anyway."

"Logan, I'm sorry. That's not at all what I pictured of your upbringing."

"Well, you're not the only one."

"That would explain a lot and why you don't want to be here."

"Exactly. But now, they want me in the business. Why now?"

"Well, can't you just say no?"

"I can, but then I wouldn't get my lovely monthly allowance." She looked annoyed. "It's easy money, Amber."

"Doesn't it bother you you're getting a free ride, though? I get value out of my job. What do you seek?"

I swiped a hand though my hair. "Seek? Are you listening to yourself? Life is hard. I don't have to do life, I get to coast. How many people would kill to be in my position?"

She looked out toward the vast landscape. "Interesting."

"Wouldn't you?"

She exhaled. "I don't know. Financial certainty is what I've always needed… wanted. I mean wanted."

She looked down to hide her face, but it was too late. I wondered why she needed it.

"Since our terrifying experience on the plane, I've been wondering… as much as I want financial freedom, is that what it's all about?"

"It is nice, I won't lie, but it's not all it is cracked up to be."

She picked up a handful of dates in a bowl. The girl had an appetite. Every pencil-thin model picked and prodded food without actually putting anything between their collagen- filled lips, but she was refreshingly different.

"Why do you want financial freedom so much, Amber? I've met no one who works the pace you do, maybe except for Carlton. But why do you want to be rich so badly?"

"Oh, that's a discussion for another day." She picked at an imaginary hair and tucked it behind her ear. "Anyway, we have loads to talk about after our meeting. Should we discuss tomorrow's visit to the mines?"

Curious to know why but sensitive to realize it was a subject she didn't want to discuss now, I left it alone for now. "I will hold you to that."

She tilted her head and settled her hand on her exposed neck. Her eyes settled on mine as she took a sharp intake of breath. "Um, so Leila has set up a satellite office for us to work from onsite. We can go there now if you've finished."

"You'll probably want to catch up with the accountants on their tour while I make some inquiries into compliance."

"Will I?"

"Yes. Won't you need help with that? I could contact the regulatory authorities and speak to them regarding the conditions."

She raised a perfectly plucked eyebrow. "You'd know how to do that?"

"Of course. Just because I'm not interested doesn't mean I lack the skill."

She smiled at me, and as the sun hit her golden face, her warm eyes stirred something in my core. Something foreign and slightly uncomfortable.

"Good to know," she said. "But I've got this covered, thanks for offering. I think you'd probably enjoy meeting up with the accountants and checking out the mining machinery. You know boys and their toys and all that…"

"If I didn't know better, I'd think you were trying to get rid of me, Ms. Anderson."

She bit her lower lip, and I saw the cracks in the polished businesswoman persona she'd so fiercely donned. "Not at all."

"Cheese?" I said, holding up another smaller container.

She checked her watch. "I should probably get back."

Was she waiting for me to convince her? She moved very slowly. Her hands splayed by her sides as she pressed herself up, her long legs outstretched on the mat with her black pencil skirt and open blouse catching the breeze.

"Or you could go back in five minutes after some delicious, non-exotic but Australian cheese."

She giggled, and it was a foreign sound coming from her. I immediately wanted to hear it again.

I cut her a slice and put it on a sesame cracker. *Dammit*, the thing broke into two.

"Shit, sorry!"

She carefully wrapped her hand around the broken cracker and her fingers grazed my thumb as she took it from me. That strange feeling resurfaced.

"It still tastes the same, broken or not."

"Does it?" I said, craving more of her touch.

She blinked before taking the entire split cracker to her rosy lips.

"See? delicious," she said. I watched her throat bob up and down, and I never wanted to be the cheese so badly as I did now. It was absolutely ridiculous but still true.

The words blurted from my lips before they could be stopped. "Is it weird to be jealous of that cheese?"

"Logan! You can't say that."

"Why, is that harassment or something?" I shrugged.

"It probably would be if we hadn't already slept together."

"I really don't see what's stopping us from doing that again. Am I the only one thinking about our time in the alleyway?"

"We can't. I'm a professional. You are the firm's client."

"Since when does that stop you from doing what you want to do?"

"I don't want to. I have my own rules, remember?"

"Fuck your rules."

"My rules are there for a reason. And what makes you think I want to sleep with you again now I know who you are?" She blinked her eyes as they darted around the picnic mat.

I exhaled. *Why did everyone assume they knew me? I was more, way more than the tabloids, wasn't I?* "Likewise, Amber." *Shit*, but that wasn't true.

She whipped her head back to me. "Well, this was a lovely trip down memory lane, but some of us have work to do."

Shit. I've pissed her off. Too bad. Two could play that game.

With quick movements, she pushed her feet into her heels and not so gracefully stood. After she smoothed down her skirt, she clutched her bag and the rest of her belongings she toted around with her.

"Has anyone ever told you, you have large feet?"

She let out a throaty, irritated groan and ignored my remark. It was a gut reaction—she'd gotten under my skin too. I picked at the cheese in front of me and knew I'd probably pushed things. The space next to me was now just a shadow of her a moment ago, cementing the fact.

The cart drove her away, and I looked over my shoulder, watching as she got smaller. She sat on the back seat, holding onto the bar. Our gazes locked until the cart disappeared around the corner.

Perhaps I'd overstepped the mark. But was it crazy to think the chemistry we shared in the alleyway was still there? There were moments, I'd see glimpses, bubbling away at the surface when she allowed herself to let her guard down.

Did I really have to be a dick all the time?

9

AMBER

I crossed my legs as the cart drove me further and further away from the lookout.

He stared, his gaze following me like an arrow flying to meet its target. The weight of it stirred something deep inside of me, but his words had cut too deep. Why wouldn't he like me? Even worse, why the heck did I care? Irritation shot from the base of my spine around to my throat culminating in a lump. A jackass one minute, then kind and sincere the next. I was Jekyll and Hyde—I didn't know who I was going to get.

The afternoon hours ticked away, turning the sunlit office to a veil of cloudy gray. I rubbed my eyes, taking care not to smudge my mascara. I shuddered at the image that came flooding in.

Black eyes.

Growing up, I'd seen it all too often with Mom. She'd said it was mascara, and I believed her when I was a kid. But the night of my eleventh birthday, when I ought to be tucked up in bed, I watched helplessly as Dad's fist slammed into her right cheek, splitting it open. I'd run into the kitchen to help, but Dad only pushed me away. Mom assured me she was fine, but the fear in her eyes told a different story. From then on, she defended Dad, telling me it wasn't his fault, and he was a good man who had anger issues. As the years ticked away and his behavior became more irrational, I begged her to leave him. She and I could run away together, but she wouldn't. In some twisted way, she still loved him. And he'd made sure she couldn't access any bank accounts. Without a job, he owned her. Her only option was to stay with him. By my eighteenth birthday, I knew I had to leave. Not only did I leave, but it was then I made sure my life would never be the same. I set rules for myself, so I could never be in a relationship.

Not knowing if one day I'd return home to find her dead plagued me every day, like fear feasting on decay. And I just couldn't do it anymore. Countless times I'd begged her to come with me, but she always refused. If Mom couldn't recognize she was in an abusive relationship, I couldn't help her. All I could do was work my damned hardest to save enough to show her there was a way out. Ever since, I hadn't stop working to do just that.

I rubbed my temples. Guilt threatened to suffocate me as I remembered sneaking out before dawn with a handful of savings and a backpack of clothes and favorite books. I breathed in slowly, the steady breath helping to calm my nerves. *Don't think about this. Not here. Not now.* But my steady breathing couldn't stop the looped nightmare.

Hiding under the table as Dad pushed Mom against the wall, his hands against her throat, wetness pricked at the back of my eyes.

"We're back." The door swung open, and Logan burst through. The sound severed the connection to my past, and I winced in my seat.

Logan took me in. "You okay?"

Trying to displace the tears that threatened to fall, I blinked and stifled a yawn. I hoped to divert his attention from my telling eyes. "Yes, perfectly fine," I said, my voice cracking slightly.

"Guys, give me a minute," Logan said to Vincent and Jacob, who appeared behind him.

"Right," Vincent huffed. Logan closed the door, so it was only him and I in the space.

Glued to my laptop screen, I typed a response to an email, but when I reread it, it was all gibberish and nonsensical. I felt his presence behind me, the heat from his body making me forget about the guilt rising in my chest. "Are you sure?" he whispered in my ear.

I took a sharp intake of breath at his proximity and of the sincerity in his voice. If I gave into the feeling pooling in my chest and let him in, it would be the end of me.

"Yes," I chided. "I'll pack up my things and meet you outside."

He sat on the desk next to me, his arm resting only inches from my hand. The weight of his stare like that of common bricks leveled at my chest.

"Well?" I stared back at him with all the courage I could muster. Yet inside, my heart banged rampantly.

He ran a hand through his full hair. "You want me to go. I'm going."

With heavy steps, he stalked out the door, then slammed it shut. I couldn't stop the knee-jerk flinch at the loud thud that followed.

Why was he annoyed?

"Ugh!" I let out an exasperated sound. I know he was only trying to help, but it was a line I couldn't cross. I quickly erased the thought of letting him in, but every time he was near, any notion of logic went out the door and the more I wanted to open up to him. Between my tempting thoughts of Logan and the terrifying images of my mother that were burned into my subconscious—the only thing keeping me sane was work.

But why now, after all this time, did I let the guilt consume me? Why now did I want to break my rules with Logan? Was it my near-death experience turning everything upside down and sideways? Did I have it all wrong this time?

* * *

The gentle hum of the luxury SUV did little to pull me away from his cologne and haphazard gazing at my thighs. Distracting myself was priority number one before my estrogen tipped the scales, and I brazenly did something I would inevitably regret. Determined to keep whatever professionalism I had left, I diverted my focus. "Did you get far today on the audit?"

"Yes, we did. Although Vincent, if I wasn't there, would have taken twice as long. The man is intolerable."

"Is he?" I grinned.

"Uh huh. We checked out the MT3300 Terex trucks."

"There's eight of them to audit, isn't there?"

His eyes widened. *Had I grown another pair of eyes?*

"Only you would remember the number, but I bet you've never seen it up close before?"

Without waiting for me to respond, he dug his hand into his suit pants, pulling out a phone that looked more banged up than my apartment on washing day. His arm touched the silk of my blouse as his warmth doused my skin. It leveled me, and suddenly, I was back in the alleyway with his strong arms wrapped around my waist, his lips possessing mine and soaking from the pouring rain. My skin burned just thinking about it.

"You sure you're, okay? You're looking a little flushed."

"Fine," I said, taking his phone and stared at the picture on the screen. The truck in the picture dwarfed him. The wheel alone was at least double his already six-foot something height. It looked like something out of *Alice in Wonderland*.

The picture vanished and was replaced with a call. "Um, *Asshole Prick* is calling," I said holding up his phone.

"Brilliant." He grabbed the phone out of my hand, and I ignored the silly buzz his fingers gave me.

"Brother," he said, putting the phone on speaker.

"Logan, where are we up to?" His brother's nasally voice filled the back of the SUV.

"How are you?" Logan asked, purposefully ignoring Carlton's question.

"Cut the bullshit. How did the meeting go today, and where are we with the compliance and audit?"

"You know you should really try some manners. I'm sure they'd help improve your business dealings. Honestly, Mommy and Daddy would be shocked!"

He laughed. "You're telling me how to run the business now? You wouldn't know how to wipe your own ass if our nanny hadn't done it for you."

I turned to see Logan's reaction. He remained still and contemplative like he was going to either stab the phone with a fork or deliver a speech to a children's orphanage. He was hovering on a dime.

"The audit is thirty percent of the way through, the machinery is as noted. No discrepancies as of yet. We have contacted the Queensland government in relation to the details in the mining leases. The compliance review and environmental authority permit is being investigated."

He'd read the many emails I'd copied him in on while onsite with Vincent and Jacob. I nearly swallowed my tongue. Logan sounded invested, intelligent, and across all of it. Something bloomed in my chest as I felt my teeth bite into the flesh of my bottom lip. His eyes drifted to mine, and instantly, the surrounding air became thick. It caused me to take a sharp intake of breath. I almost forgot he was on a phone call. I mustered a smile back.

"Fine. I'll call you tomorrow," Carlton said.

His brother's voice sounded down the line, interrupting whatever we had going on. But then something shifted in Logan's indigo eyes. The sadness held behind his eyes appeared again, if only momentarily.

Logan shifted his gaze back to the phone resting on his leg. "Wait. Did you sign off on the beach house?"

"No. And I won't. You need to be close to all the action."

"That's bullshit, and you know it. You're not signing it off because you want to control me." Logan pulled at his collar, trying to loosen the grip it had around his neck.

"Yeah, maybe that's it." A wicked laugh sounded down the line.

"Fuck you," Logan spat and hung up.

For the rest of the drive, we sat in silence, and as the SUV pulled up to our cabins, I leaped out, making my way toward the door.

The SUV accelerated away as he appeared next to me.

"You were upset this afternoon. Can I attempt to make you dinner?" he asked, walking beside me.

"You seem like you had a terrible phone call. Maybe I'm the one that should offer."

"I'm stuck at this place for the foreseeable future because my dearest brother won't sign off on a house by the beach."

"There aren't any beaches near here?"

"And that's why they invented helicopters."

I burst into laughter. "Oh God, you're serious? You hate this place so much you'd spend thousands of dollars trading a roof over your head? Then a helicopter to fly you in and out each day?"

"Trading roofs?" He lifted his chin toward the tangerine skyline. "That's an interesting way to look at it. When you say it like that, it does seem a little…"

"Selfish?" I threw out the first word that sprung to mind.

"I was going to say dickish." He split a grin, and I couldn't help but laugh.

"You know I envy that about you."

"What's that?" he asked.

"You tell it like it is. I used to be like that, but I've learned now I need to have a filter to be successful, especially in a man's world."

"Why filter anything? People either love me or they hate me. And I never truly know because of my name. They all appear to love me because of the Magma name. It gets boring and lonely."

"Filters are important." *Lonely? He gets lonely?*

"No, they are not," he counterpunched.

"They keep us safe."

"Like your rules?" He stared at me, rays of chemistry passing between us.

"Yes, exactly like them." I jingled the keys in my hand.

"So, yours or mine?" he asked.

"What?" My cheeks burned.

"For dinner, Amber." He grinned, and his hooded eyes held onto mine like Gorilla Glue.

"Y… yes. Right. Y… yours," I stuttered out like an imbecile. "What time?"

"How about I just tap on the wall when it's ready?"

"Either that or I can smell my way over." I shook my head. "Sorry, that was lame."

His mouth tipped into a smile that pinched at his nose. "Not at all."

"Well… I'll ah… see you later, I guess…" I shook my head as I shoved the key into the lock. Quickly, I shut the door behind me and took two steps forward. I propelled myself onto the bed from exhaustion. It didn't help I was a blithering mess.

Veiled in the earlier imagery of my mother had weighed me down. Usually, the guilt reared its head when I had a spare moment to think about her. But lately, it had been more frequent. So why did I commit to dinner? *Because you couldn't refuse him.*

After berating myself over my barely controlled attraction to the man, I did the next best thing—work. I leaned over the edge of the bed, reached into my briefcase, and pulled out my laptop.

The screen flickered to white, and as I waited for it to load, I wondered if my earlier inquiries had responded. At the same time, I also wondered if maybe another tryst with Logan was what I needed. Just to forget.

What about your rules, Amber?

The internal struggle my brain had with my body did nothing to help, so I typed an email to my boss, Chadwick. For a moment, it would take my focus off Logan's half-hooded eyes and athletic body.

After ten minutes, I clicked send. *Great, now what?*

After I unbuttoned my blouse and peeled it down my arms, I unzipped my pencil skirt and freed it from my waist, letting it fall to the ground. With the weight of my clothes now gone, I stared at my reflection in the mirror. Only once had a man ever seen me naked in the light of day. Anything more than that, and I'd risk falling into the trap of my parents' relationship. But, as I stared at my long legs in the mirror, I thought of the ease at which he held me in place as they scissored around him in the alleyway, and I couldn't help but wonder what a relationship with Logan would be like.

My thoughts seemed to circle back to Logan. I walked to the shower and adjusted the water until it was some kind of blistering normal and stepped in. I let the water engulf me, throwing my head forward as it cascaded down my back. The lackluster fan did little to quell the swells of steam clouding the bathroom. I scrubbed my collarbone, torso, and legs, trying to absolve myself from guilt that currently rushed back to the surface. The guilt that had never left since the day I deserted my mother and left her with a monster five years ago. The cold shower alerted me it was time to step out, but as hard as I scrubbed, the guilt remained.

Where was my mother now? Was she still with him? Of course, Amber. Reaching out wasn't an option. It was too late for that, wasn't it?

When I was done drying off, I wrapped the towel snugly around me, knotting it in the corner and walked over to the closet. I stared at the options I'd unpacked and flicked through the sea of black and white corporate clothing. They wouldn't do. I'd packed two dresses, one a loose navy dress with a neckline that showed a swell of cleavage. *Maybe.* I flicked the hanger across the metal rod. *Ah, it had to be this one*—a bone white dress that cinched in at the waist and bust and fell just above the knee. It showed every curve and would send the completely wrong message. If I could withstand him in this dress, then there'd be no worries for the rest of the trip.

Setting a challenge for myself would be a proper distraction. Something to work toward. Besides, I'd always liked a challenge. It was easier to succeed in my opinion. I picked up my headband and got changed. When I was done, I stared at myself in the mirror, trying to remember why I'd set the challenge of dressing to impress. Because in this dress, I would wake the living dead.

My phone sounded from the other side of the room. I scurried across the bed to reach for it on the bedside table. Lily's name flashed up on the screen.

"Lil, hey!"

"You all right?" she asked.

"Yeah, just leaped over the bed." I pulled on the hem of my dress that had scrunched up my thighs.

"Wish I was a fly on the wall to see that. Just seeing how your day is going, I miss you!"

"It's only been a few days since dinner, Lil!"

"True. So, how is it?"

"Well, apart from the plane's engine failure, and my direct report turned out to be the guy I slept with in alleyway… it's fucking wonderballs."

"Back up, back up. Are you okay? *Shit!* Amber, why didn't you call me after what happened on the plane?"

"I'm okay, I think. It's just been full-on."

"Maybe you should step back and process that for a minute."

Since when have I ever processed anything?

"And who's the guy?"

I lowered my voice, in case the thin walls betrayed me. "Remember the guy that bought us a round of drinks at dinner?"

"Yes." She paused. "No!" she gasped. "When you went back in to get your jacket?"

"He was there."

"In the alleyway?"

"It wasn't my finest moment, but we didn't exactly make it back to my place." I grinned.

"Well, it sounds like you both couldn't help yourself!" She giggled before abruptly stopping. "Hang on, now you're working together?"

"Yes, he's Logan Magma."

"You slept with a Magma brother?"

"Yes. I didn't know. Anyway, now, it's purely business."

"God, you and your rules." She sighed, and even I hated the redundancy in my voice.

"Me and my rules have gotten me this far."

"No, you and hard work is what you got you there."

"Have you ever wondered what it's all for, Lily?" I picked at the invisible lint on my dress.

"What do you mean?"

"I don't know, I think the plane incident is really messing with me."

"Like, why you have all those fucking rules?"

"You know why I have those rules."

"I know why, but you know I don't agree with them." Silence rang down the line.

"Enough about me. What are you doing, Lil? How's the flower shop?"

"Busy! I can't keep up. Blake says I should hire an assistant."

"Maybe he's onto something there."

"Or maybe he just wants me all to himself on the weekends."

I laughed. Since Blake returned to Seaview, Lily had been the most settled and happy I'd ever seen. Now, they were planning a life together.

"Again, maybe he's onto something there!" Laughter echoed the line, and as much as I wanted to stay and chat, I had to go. "Hey, Lil, I have to run. I'm having dinner with Logan."

"Logan Magma, the guy who's purely business, not the best-sex-in-the-alleyway guy?"

"That's the one. Okay, I'll call you when I'm back in Seaview."

"Amber—" She wanted to talk more, wanted to flesh out whatever was going on with Logan and me, but I couldn't for fear of what I'd say or not say.

"Bye, Lil!" I quickly interrupted her before she could finish.

I pressed *End* on the phone and walked toward the door. I twisted the ends of my hair, but it did little to quell the nerves butterflying around in my stomach.

10

LOGAN

"Why did you invite me over when you can't cook?" She pressed her hand into the arc of her hip.

"You're right, I'm hopeless." She'd worn a white dress, so unsubtly sexy I had a hard time keeping my eyes off her since opening the door. It clung to her curvy hips and her narrow waist, and that ass so deliciously round and perky, it was a felony I couldn't touch it.

I'd picked a crisp dove-blue shirt with the sleeves rolled up and dark denim jeans and maybe spent a bit too much time on my hair rather than attempting dinner.

"Never fear, I've paid a ridiculous amount for dinner to be delivered. I can't guarantee it will be warm, though, by the time it gets here."

"How did you manage that? Is there even a restaurant near here?"

"Kind of, it's an hour away."

"Well, I don't know about you, but cold food doesn't appeal to me."

"What does appeal to you?" The hollow of her neck sucked inward as she inhaled sharply.

An untimely knock at the door pulled me away from leaning in and kissing her neck.

"I'll get it." She bolted upright from the opposite end of the lounge where she had perched herself. I noticed it was the furthest spot from me.

I watched her as she walked the long way around so as not to pass me to get to the front door.

"Well, hello there." The guy at the door flagrantly eye-fucked her top to toe. If he didn't cut it out, the last thing he'd see would be stars.

The vein in my neck throbbed. I moved beside her to calm my agitation. "I got it, Amber." My hand pressed on the exposed part of her back between the shoulder blades, and under my palm, I felt her quickened breath.

"Okay," she whispered as she slipped past me.

The buff delivery boy wore a tank top, a local surfer boy from the coast no doubt, earning extra bucks driving food delivery. One after another, he handed over the paper bags in silence. I ignored the stolen glances toward Amber.

"Here. Keep the change." I handed him the wad of bills from my jeans' pocket.

He stared at it like it was his lucky fucking day.

"Thanks, man," he exclaimed.

And here I was, hoping that measly tip would annoy him.

"If you hadn't gawked at the lady like the horny teenager you are, you would have gotten way more."

His eyes widened at the same time his jaw dropped. That's when I slammed the door shut. I turned around, and Amber had positioned herself on the furthest end of the lounge again, her shocked expression mirrored his. "What?"

She narrowed her eyes. "He can gawk if he wants to. What's it to you?"

Her hazel eyes, framed in lashes, called me to a challenge.

"I enjoy gawking at you," I said, responding to her call. *Two can play at this game, sweetheart.*

She cleared her throat, a pink blush creeping up her neck. A color I was now becoming quite fond of.

"Well, don't. Gosh, do you know how annoying you are!"

She stood and paced, her cool exterior wavering by the second. With confusion, I watched her. She appeared like she had her own internal battle going on, fighting against herself. What was I going to do about these goddamn rules of hers and this pent-up, back-and-forth banter we continued to have? As much as I respected her for her dedication to her job, I couldn't understand why she denied herself something she obviously wanted.

Abruptly, I interrupted her pacing and handed her one of the bags. It appeared we both needed a distraction.

"Well, what do we have here?" She unwrapped a bag and eyeballed the contents inside.

"Oh, yum!" She pulled out the oysters I'd ordered.

"I hope you like seafood."

"Who doesn't?"

I puffed out my cheeks. "You'd be surprised," I said, leaving the wonder hanging in the air.

"At least you have an appetite. I love that."

"Absolutely no problem there. I'm the type of girl who licks the plate clean."

"Of course, you are." I pressed my lips into a slight smile.

Her rules. Why had she never broken them? Why did she have them?

And fuck, if she bent over anymore in that dress, I'd have to chain myself to the wall. "Can't say I know too many girls like that."

In the dingy cabin with the moldy carpet and old drapes as window furnishings, we sat at the rickety table, demolishing our plates piled with Pacific oysters, shrimp, and lobster.

She tilted a shell and slid the oyster into her open mouth.

An audible groan threatened to leave my lips as I watched her swallow it down.

My hands ached with a need to touch her.

"I bet you know a lot of girls," she said.

"I bet you know a lot of guys."

She tipped her full lips into a smile. "Touché. And you're wondering what that makes me?"

"Not at all." I shot back.

With one hand, she reached up and lightly clasped at her neck.

"Why should men be able to sleep around but women can't?" I, of all people, couldn't judge with the amount of pussy I've had over the years.

She shrugged. "My thoughts exactly."

"But men do it because we like no strings attached. I wonder if your reasons are different. I wonder if you were hurt so badly from a past relationship, that it's stopping you from finding happiness ever again… and if that's the case, I want to know who the bastard is and make sure he can never hurt you or anyone else ever again."

She scratched at the blush on her neck, "Um, look, I don't want to—"

"Tell me I'm wrong, Amber."

She blinked like rapid fire, and her shoulders straightened. "If we're being so observant… you pretend not to care about this deal, but I'm not buying it."

"No?" I asked with a raised brow.

"No."

"You're deflecting," I said.

"So are you, Logan. You read my email."

"Huh?"

"In the SUV, you updated your brother. You could have only done that if you read my emails."

"Which email was that? You sent six in under an hour. You keep working at that pace, you'll end up with an embolism."

"And you keep pretending to have no brains and zero interest in anything, you'll push your family further away."

I put my napkin down and titled my head. She saw me. Not the man with the Magma name, but the real me.

Suddenly, I wanted to hold her and make both our pain melt away in each other's arms—more than anything, more than fucking the money-hungry hangers-on and the wafer-thin models. That was my past. I leaned across my elbows, my face inches apart from hers.

"And you think there's more to me than that?"

"I do. Yes." She cleared her throat. "By the way, this seafood is delicious but such a waste. You should really learn how to cook, especially when there's a fridge full of food."

"I'll keep that in mind. Amber?"

"Yes," she breathed.

"I may not know what happened, but I know one thing. When we're together, I know you want to break your rules."

She wrapped both hands around the curve of the plate, using it as her support crutch. "Logan, I can't."

"That wasn't a no."

She pushed the chair back and straightened, giving me her back.

"Amber, wait, where are you going?" She dropped her plate in the sink. It clinked like cheap china.

"I really should go."

Before I could string a sentence together, she'd already crossed the threshold.

* * *

Another mind-numbing day of compliance and audits kept me busy. I could do the work, but did I love it? Hell, no. I'd rather tongue a flame thrower. *But in all fairness, did I like anything?*

I reflected to the summer of 2015 in Nice—a bar, too many cocktails, and the CEO of an organization for cancer for kids betting me twenty grand on a game of pool. After spending a day on the yacht on the turquoise waters of the Cote D'Azur, he'd cornered me, and I'd accepted willingly because I had the confidence a shitload of liquor could bring. And then I lost. But instead of pocketing the money, he asked if I would sponsor the upcoming charity ball for kids with brain cancer. What a fucking eye-opener, meeting eight-year-old Sierra, who'd just discovered her cancer was terminal. Looking into her innocent eyes made my childhood look like a never-ending ticket to Disneyland.

But amongst all the fear and sadness at that ball, there was an undertone of hope. I felt an overwhelming pull of reward, knowing the money raised could help fund more research or help parents take time off from work to be there for their kids.

Maybe there was something there worth exploring.

With that thought, I found I was completely uninterested in what was happening with this deal once again. Keeping myself distracted, I checked my watch as we stood auditing another CAT. I held the groan that threatened to escape my lips and diverted my focus onto Amber's coal-black skirt that clung to her curves. The autumn rays burned stronger here than the coastline, and I shifted my attention to her tightly wrapped bun and noticed how her brown hair reflected patinas of auburns under the midday sun.

Her commanding presence, purposely led by her own clear set of goals and direction, made me envy her. I watched her with Vincent and Jacob. Professional and polished, she was so far removed from the after-five Amber. Since her, my wayward existence had come into question.

Last night, she'd left me with blue balls and an insane but undeniable wanting. So unbearable that a *do it yourself* in the shower with only her white dress and hazel eyes on my mind was barely enough to keep me contained.

"Are you listening?" She elbowed me, and without me realizing, had extracted herself from the others and appeared by my side.

I leaned down, bringing my mouth close to her ear. "Kind of."

She turned to me. Her teeth dragged across the bottom of her peachy lips, and our eyes met. Her heady eyes lulling me into submission.

"Actually, I was thinking about jetting off to the Amalfi after this deal is done. Want to be my plus one?"

"You've got to be…" She shook her head and strutted away.

Noticing the nerdy minds entertained around the excavator, I clawed at her arm, jerking her back.

I kept my voice low. "I know you want what I gave you in Seaview."

A blush crept up her neck, but this time she didn't look at me.

I released her arm, and she smoothed down her hair that led into her top bun. "Vincent, can you confirm the CAT working order matches the specifications sheet?"

Vincent, like a boy in the front row of class, checked his clipboard. "Yes. It all matches, as it should."

Bored with this audit and the one-sided flirting, I checked my phone. An email from my brother flashed unread in my inbox. I clicked on it, and the first thing I noticed was he'd carbon copied Dad in on the same email. *Great.*

Last time I'd spoken to Dad was before I left Perth to come here. His words were like a skid mark on the road, a permanent reminder of the man who disowned me from early on.

"Your mother wanted you back, not me, not your brother. Don't fuck this deal up, Logan."

Not even bothering to read it, I locked my phone. *Why drag me back here now? Why threaten to cut my allowance now?* Being a nomad, far away from Perth, and away from the family suited us both, especially since no one thought I had the chops to work at Magma anyway. No one, except Mother whose guilt finally caught up with her for pushing me away at such a young age.

A piercing high-pitched noise echoed throughout the transport area of the mine and cut me away from my thoughts.

"What the hell is that?" I yelled.

Jacob and Vincent exchanged glances I took little notice of until my eyes crashed into Ambers. The same fear on the plane was behind them. Quickly, I walked to be by her side, but before I could say anything, Leila appeared. "Everyone, please follow me."

"What's going on?" I asked.

"Just listen for once, Logan, please," Amber blurted, gathering her folders to put into her briefcase.

"You're going to have to leave that, Amber. We have to evacuate, now." Leila's voice was polite yet stern.

"You heard the lady." I reached over and grabbed Amber's hand, stopping her from packing her belongings. Her gaze met mine, fragility and confusion etched in her eyes.

"Okay." Immediately she put everything down as I steered her toward the evacuation point. Vincent and Jacob already streaked ahead of Leila, not giving their belongings a second thought. Or us for that matter.

After a few minutes, a hundred or so people had congregated. Leila was chatting with the Operations Manager, Taylor, while Burt, the General Manager, was busy on the phone.

The mine workers and administration chatted in hushed voices, formed groups, and sat on the odd square of grass. To the right of a group of workers in their hardhats, Amber sat with Vincent and Jacob on the stone rock wall. Her body, although still, had lost some of its rigidness.

I meandered through the crowd, not wanting to be away from her any more than necessary, but a tap on the shoulder caught my attention.

"You must be *the* Mr. Magma buying this place?"

"Call me Logan, mate, and it's the family, not me per se." I extended my arm, but he held his blackened hands up.

"Mining hands," he said.

"A bit of dirt never hurt anyone," I said, keeping my arm extended.

He took it, nodding. "I'm Jim. Jim Brown. I've been working at this Danker Mine for twenty-two years."

He was dressed in miner's overalls with full length pants and steel-toed boots laced with orange laces that matched his orange hardhat.

"Guess you must love it then?"

He shook his head. "Nah, but the coins, good. I need the money for my sick daughter." He waved his hand, and a look of embarrassment covered his face. "Sorry, I didn't say that because I know you're rich, I really didn't." He rubbed his forehead, smearing the black dirt into a thick line across his skin.

"Mate, of all people, you don't strike me as the gold-digging type… pardon the pun."

His laugh was lion loud as he slapped his belly. "Good one!"

"What's wrong with your daughter, if you don't mind me asking?"

"A.L.L or Acute lymphoblastic leukemia. She's had it since she was three. In and out of hospitals." He shook his head. "She's nine now, and the bastard cancer just came back again. We're just lucky she's a fighter."

"Fucking cancer, if only we could eradicate it altogether. Everyone knows someone who has had it. I can't imagine what that must be like as a parent watching her suffer like that."

"It's knowing you can't do a thing that's the hardest part." He lifted the back of his hand to wipe his eyes.

My heart constricted. I reached over and patted him on the back. "What can I do to help, Jim?"

"Nothing. Sorry, I don't know where that came from. I think I see Burt about to speak," he said and tilted his head in Burt's direction.

"Everyone, quiet down, please." Burt's voice cut through the already hushed chatter.

I side glanced at Jim, who had opened up to me more than I'd ever seen my dad even dare to. He clearly was in pain, his face tight and constricted. Surely, work could cover him so he could support his daughter in her treatment?

"Ladies and gentlemen, thank you for your patience. There was a minor gas leak in chamber two of the open pit. We have our engineers looking into it as we speak, but keeping with protocol, there will be no work for the rest of the day."

A few whistles and cheers came from the crowd.

"All right, settle down. We will be in touch about tomorrow as soon as we hear from the preliminary reports."

"Well, that suits me just fine," I said to no one in particular.

"Wow, that's the third leak this year. I'm going to take this opportunity to Skype my sweet Ella before her treatment tomorrow. Nice to meet you, Logan."

Third leak? "Likewise, and best of luck with your daughter, Jim."

The crowd dispersed quicker than kids around an empty pinata.

I waited for Amber as she finished talking with Taylor and Leila.

"Bye, Logan," Jacob said as Vincent hopped into the waiting car.

"Where are you staying?" I asked Vincent.

"In Hopetown, there was one house left. I got my assistant to book it."

"Well, aren't you lucky," I said.

"Where are you?" Vincent asked, lowering the window as his driver shut the door.

"In the fucking fly-in, fly-out cabins."

"No, you're not!" Vincent laughed, only reining it in after realizing it wasn't the joke of the year.

"Yeah."

"Why don't you stay in the city and fly in, it would only be twenty minutes, wouldn't it?"

"You know that asshole brother of mine. Actually, I think you know him well."

Vincent stilled. I'd gathered they'd worked together for over ten years, so he knew him very well. And his loyalty was very much with Carlton and not me.

"Oh, I'm sure he had his reasons."

Case and point. *Fuck off.*

Vincent blinked rapidly, then turned, presumably signaling the driver because the black SUV immediately accelerated. He waved goodbye, his mouth set in a straight line. I didn't trust the guy, and I sure as hell didn't enjoy him being here. *Fuck him and fuck Carlton, whatever those two bunnies had going on.*

Amber walked toward me. If her ears could let out steam, they would be smokestacks.

"What's wrong?"

"I can't get my laptop, that's what's wrong. They won't let me in!"

"And?"

"And I have a ton of work to do."

"No, you don't."

In my peripheral vision, our SUV came toward us, quicker than normal. I pulled at her waist as she crashed into me. She stared up at me, her eyes reflecting the afternoon sun, turning them a shade of caramel with pops of emerald green. I drank her in like a cocktail, equal parts intoxicating and suffocating.

"Sorry, I didn't want to add getting squashed by a car to our trip as well."

"Thank you," she breathed but stayed still.

In case of prying eyes, I let go, and she looked down. "It's a beautiful day, you don't have your laptop, and we can't do any work…"

"So?" Her lusty eyes pulled me to focus.

"Wait here. I have an idea." I walked over to the driver's side of the SUV. The driver did a double take before sliding down the window, the cool air from inside flowing out.

"Mr. Magma, what can I do for you?"

"How's five-hundred bucks for the afternoon off?" I peeled open my wallet, not so discreetly handing over the hundreds.

"You don't have to ask me twice," he said.

I held the money tight. "There's a catch. I need the car."

"It's yours," he said immediately.

When I released my grip on the cash, he unbuckled his seat belt and jumped out.

"Just don't tell anyone, Mr. Magma."

"I won't if you won't." I winked, and he grinned, then he took off on foot in the opposite direction.

Jumping into the driver's side, I shifted into gear and reversed, appearing beside Amber. I lowered the passenger window. Amber's gaze intently fixed on mine. "Ah, where is our driver?"

"You're looking at him." I grinned.

"Logan, what did you do?"

"You're taking the afternoon off. Boss's orders."

"Boss?" She narrowed her eyes.

"Technically, we both know I am, but I'm not playing that card."

"Maybe you should." She hopped into the passenger seat.

"You would like that, wouldn't you?" I asked, pressing the accelerator and leaving a dust bowl in our wake.

"I'd like it if you paid more attention to the deal rather than chatting with every Tom, Dick, and Harry here."

I put my seat belt on. "I met Jim, not Tom or Dick."

"Ugh, you know what I mean." She folded her arms across her chest. "Jim's daughter has cancer. She's nine."

"Oh. That's awful."

I nodded. "Yep, and what's worse, he's stuck here not able to be by her side while she's at the hospital getting treatment."

"Money, it's a real thing, you know," she said flatly.

"So, I hear." I grinned, and she rolled her eyes.

"I'm going to help him."

She whipped her head toward me. "How?"

"Don't know yet." I changed lanes with ease and realized I missed driving myself around.

"No offense, but why?"

"I shrugged. Don't know why, but I need to."

I paused. "Maybe it's because as a kid, I didn't have the support of my parents and had I had that, things might have been different. Or maybe because the one time I gave money to any kind of charity, it made me feel important and valued. I guess you'd say it's selfish."

I turned to her as my grip on the steering wheel stretched the skin around my knuckles.

She smiled. "It is, but any charity work where you both can benefit is a win in my eyes." She reached up into her bun and untwisted it, letting it fall to her shoulders. "By the way, where are we going? I have nothing with me. No purse, documents, laptop. Nada!"

"It's a surprise," I said, glimpsing at her relaxed and wildly tousled hair.

"Logan, come on. I hate surprises."

"Oh, well."

"Oh, well?" Her voice rose an active.

"Cool your stilettos. It's a place I read about, about thirty minutes from here. You think you can last that long, or do I need to distract you?" Her eyes held mine like magnets as her shy smile dissolved into her cheeks.

"I can last," she said, taking in a big influx of air through her teeth.

11

AMBER

The more his dark eyes ran over me, the more I dissolved, piece by piece, like ice into water. And the frustration brewing inside of me these past few days had moved from the nape of my neck to the pit of my belly.

For the time being, my rules were keeping me safe, but sitting alongside him en route to a surprise location scared me. For two reasons—trusting myself around him was proving more difficult by the day, and two, I'd never ever taken time off work before. But with the evacuation order in place, no equipment to audit and no emails to follow up without my laptop, I technically couldn't do anything other than ruminate.

Wherever we were going, I guess we could discuss work issues. But as I ran my eyes over his thick, firm thighs and muscular arms, I doubted that. The more I resisted him, the more I needed to have him, the more I craved him.

The car slowed, and he expertly pulled into a narrow area between two Banksia trees.

"We're here."

I glanced around. Shrubs, tall trees with towering foliage, and crushed gravel surrounded us. "Where's here exactly?"

"You'll see." His lips split into a lopsided grin.

I rolled my eyes, but even I couldn't ignore the butterflies soaring in my belly.

When I opened the car door, the humidity rushed into the air-conditioned SUV. Unseasonably warm and muggy for autumn, my blouse had already begun to stick to my skin. I untucked it, bunny eared both sides, so that it knotted just above my belly button. Satisfied with my make-do top, I peered up only to find him opposite me, staring.

The cracks of heat exploded between us again, and this time, like a game of cat and mouse, he was the first to break away. He unhooked his cufflinks and rolled his sleeves up over his elbows, his bicep muscles tightened underneath his vanilla white shirt.

The heat had me all in a fizz, but I wasn't so sure it was the heat.

"Shall we? It's down that pathway." He gestured.

Surrounded by century-old trees and a paved pathway carpeted with fallen golden brown leaves, it was as though we were in the middle of a rainforest. Stepping out of my black patent pumps, I hooked them around my fingers, wanting to feel the bare earth on my feet. Both sides of the pathway were lined with palm trees, while tropical plants created a rainbow arch of shade that led—actually I didn't know where it led to. Instead of walking the middle path, I stepped on the edges of the pavers, finding comfort in the uniformity.

On the drive, Logan has convinced me to close my eyes whenever a sign was drawing up ahead. He was hell bent on not to give away the location. And I, uncharacteristically, let go of my sass to keep the surprise. And I couldn't round out an excuse quick enough back at Danker Gold to get out of it. I wondered if he'd surprised anyone special to him before. Had he had many girlfriends? The quick google search I did on my boss didn't pull up anything too serious. Just a string of gorgeous women, the type with a gene pool from the likes of Sean Connery and Audrey Hepburn, and a few photos of a pretty girl in his hometown of Perth. But he'd wanted to take *me* here.

"I like this look." He peered over at me.

"What look is that exactly?"

"It's the casual, easy-going, not-about-to-put-my-balls-in-a-vice Amber."

I dissolved into laughter. "Ah, that look. But technically, you're meant to be the one holding that vice."

"If only that were true. You've had me since the alleyway, Amber. No suit is going to change that." His gaze lifted me to another sphere. I swallowed, but the lump didn't lift from my throat. I wobbled, losing my balance, and nearly deviating from finding the edge of a paver.

"You're not going all Rafael Nadal on me, are you?"

I laughed, and it sounded higher than usual. "How did you notice that? You must think I'm a weirdo."

"I notice a lot of things about you, but it's the why I have trouble with. Like, why you step on the lines and avoid the center of the paver?" he asked as though he held a genuine interest.

I shrugged. "Something to do." That's not true. My rules and routines keep me safe. Keep me from ever going back to where I came from.

"You got to give me more than that, Amber."

The sound of gushing water diverted both our attention. "Down there, look." He reached his hand out toward mine but pulled away at the last second. Not like I would've taken it, anyway, but his action stung like a swarm of wasps.

Through the thick foliage of the emerald-green forest, several waterfalls came into view. The creek bed was dotted with enormous shiny black boulders, some bigger than a small home, with waterfalls cascaded into several smaller-tiered pools. Magical didn't even begin to describe it.

"Wow, is this—"

"Welcome to Babinda Boulders. Isn't she a treat?" Logan said.

"This is Babinda Boulders? I've always wanted to come here. Isn't this known as the Devil's Pools? And aren't those boulders made from granite? And Logan, look up there…" I pointed in the distance to the huge waterfall, not caring if I sounded like a kid who inherited a candy shop, "… I think that's the main waterfall from Mt. Bartle Frere that feeds the creek."

"For someone that's never been here, you sure know a lot about it. Why haven't you?"

"Between finishing my law degree and throwing myself into full-time work, I haven't had the chance."

"That's no excuse."

"Yes, it is. Work and study are perfectly reasonable excuses!" I said, whipping my head toward him. "Um… and what is it you think you're doing?"

He'd already unbuttoned his shirt, the peak of his chest, muscular and hard like the boulders in front of me, tempted me to slide my hands all over it. He threw his shirt on the rock, then unzipped his trousers. *I should look away.*

"What does it look like I'm doing?"

In a quick motion, he'd lowered his designer pants, so they fell around his ankles. Sculptured lower abs and obliques tapered to delicious V-lines had me spilling over with lust.

Rules. Rules. Rules!

"But…"

"Don't pretend you haven't seen it before." He stepped out of his pants, not noticing the wet sand on them. He stood taller than me, naked, except for his Calvin Klein undies that barely kept everything in. His legs were muscular and rock solid.

Every cell in my body suddenly switched on, acutely remembering those legs supporting my weight as he took me against the rough wall, his lips on my neck, and the way his hooded eyes made me his under the starry sky.

What I hadn't noticed during our moonlit tryst was the ink on the side of his abdominal muscles. "Is that Sanskrit?"

"Man Manayatey."

"Come again?"

"All this talking, not enough action!" Instantly, he leaped forward from the sandy edge and plunged into the water head on. His muscular body in a freestyle graceful movement glided through the crystal-clear waters. After a minute, he surfaced, throwing his head back, sending water droplets flying high. His hair all spikey and lush, begged for a comb or my hand.

"Ah, this is amazing. What are you waiting for?" he yelled.

"Unlike you, I'm just wearing a thong."

He swam toward me. "I think you're forgetting I've seen it all before."

It looked refreshing. I sighed, wondering if I could I trust myself enough to stay away from him.

"What if someone comes?"

He turned his head left, then right, and I realized how silly I'd sounded when we were in the middle of nowhere. I laughed. Again, he'd cornered me, and I'd run out of excuses. I wanted to dive right in, head first, and forget about how I repeatedly watched Dad as he hurt Mom and the guilt of leaving her in that situation for the last five years hadn't left me. I could forget, if only for the afternoon. "Just for a quick dip then."

Thankful for the white lace bra I'd picked this morning instead of my sports bra, I untied the loop of my blouse and unbuttoned the first few buttons. Just enough to scoop it over my head. When I glanced up at him, he turned around as soon as he'd seen I'd caught him staring.

"Bit late for that, isn't it?"

"Maybe. But I was trying to respect your rules you are so hell-bent on following."

Another pang of disappointment shot through me. *Why do I want him to?*

Careful not to muddy it on the sandy bank, I slipped down my skirt and placed it on top of a nearby rock. Dressed in a white thong and barely-there bra, I dived in. The crisp, cool water instantly struck my sticky skin and effectively lowered my body temperature—a welcome feeling after witnessing him undress.

Keeping myself at a safe distance, I swam past him and headed toward the waterfall. My fingers glided through the water, and I watched as the crystal-clear water peeled back over my hands.

After a few moments, I stopped against a boulder to catch my breath. I couldn't remember when I'd last done any exercise, but I knew sitting at a desk for ten plus hours each day hadn't done me any favors. As my breath returned to normal, I admired the clearest waters that fed the tiered waterholes.

In this moment, I easily escaped the frustration I felt around Logan. His charm couldn't irk or tempt me as I absorbed the tranquility I felt here. Just the thought of him had me looking for him, but as I did a quick scan, I couldn't see him anywhere. *It was for the best anyway.* But even at the thought, I wondered where he'd gone.

Leaning with my back on the sun-heated boulder, its smooth surface was like a hot stone massage, and the warmth was therapeutic against my bare behind. After a few minutes, I climbed out of the water and sat on the rock face, the gushing water falling down my hair and shoulders.

Out of nowhere, I heard Logan's voice echo around the creek bed. "Watch this." I stretched my neck over the boulder ledge to look in the lower pools but couldn't' see him. Not knowing where else to look, I stood. His face, fresh and wild as he stood on a boulder above, caught my eye. *Did he pass me without me seeing?*

He sat down on the rock which must have been six or seven yards long and gradually dropped off into a small pool of water below it. He slid on the sheet of water as it cascaded below him, creating a natural waterslide and crashed into the pool—sheets of water flying up around him.

"Yewww! That was brilliant!"

"You're crazy," I yelled out.

"Your turn," he said, motioning me to try it. Hell, it looked like a blast. I'd always been one of those kids who envied the kids allowed to go to an amusement park. I'd never been. Dad would never allow Mom to take me on her own, he controlled the money, so he controlled her. And he was always too busy to ever want to spend time with me.

"Coming," I said as I took the longer, safer way up the rock face.

He watched me as I rounded the waterfall above him, my half nakedness on full display like the rocks that lay before us. I placed myself on top of the rock and extended my legs, bracing myself by extending an arm. With a light grip, I held on to a nearby, higher rock ledge.

"Let go!" he yelled.

My hand obeyed and released the rock, sending my body in a free-flowing descent down the rock face. As I plunged into the water, my feet were the first to make contact. When I broke the surface, I pushed my hair off my face and saw Logan as he stood in the pool of water. Beads of water trickled down the valleys of his muscles, and my eyes followed the movement. My heart rate quickened, and I quickly shifted my focus to his face.

I grinned. "That was amazing!"

His smile stilled. His eyes darkened. But he didn't make a move.

My heart, like an explosion of fireworks, pounded in my chest.

Move away, Amber. I heard my thoughts, but my legs betrayed me by taking a step toward him. I needed to change the course of my thoughts.

I cleared my throat. "I like how you want to help Jim."

He closed the gap and tilted my chin. "I like you."

I sucked in a breath. "Do you?" I asked, jutting out my hip.

"Don't play with me, Amber."

"Logan." I breathed. "We can't."

"I dare you to bend your rules." His eyes blazed.

I dug my teeth into my lower lip, hard enough it nearly drew blood. *Touch me. Kiss me.* But my internal pleas remained unanswered as he kept me at arm's length. The water flowed between our half-naked bodies. The wind swirled and leaves rustled against the backdrop of moss-covered boulders and trickling waterfalls, and suddenly, none of it mattered. An insatiable need purged from within, and with all thinking aside, I leaned in, pressing my wet lips to his. I wrapped my hands around the base of his neck and kissed him with the same gravity only he could fulfill. My skin tingled and heated against the brisk water. I felt his hand between my shoulders, the other wrapped across the swell of my hip, dragging me toward him. A rush of blood fired through me, pooling between my legs as he pressed his hardness into my lace panties. I pushed my breasts against his chest, wanting to feel all of him.

"Amber, what are you doing to me?" His hands palmed my ass. His kiss turned hot and desperate like the burning sun. He raked his tongue down my chin and jaw, tracing my neck with languid, fervent kisses. The apex of my thighs heated. My skin, hot like lava. *Fuck any of the rules.* I wanted him, now.

As though reading my mind, he thumbed his shorts down his legs while I flung off my lace thong. His hand traced to the back of my bra and in an instant, he'd unclasped it. "I want to see all of you," he said, his eyes dark.

He wrapped his mouth over my nipple while his fingers entered me. His breath was hot and wet as he teased me with his tongue. His sucking was sweet and tortuous, and I closed my eyes, feeling everything building inside me.

"Jesus," I cried, barely able to take what he was giving me. I curled my fingers around his thick hair and held him like a lifeline.

He lifted me against the boulder, our bodies half out of the water. He erection dug into my thigh, and I parted for him like the Red Sea. He took two fingers inside me, expertly circling my clit while fingering me, and the feeling made every cell in my body awaken from a lifelong coma. I pulled at his hair, the intensity almost bringing me to the brink.

"Logan." I breathed in his ear.

"Amber, fuck, I've wanted you every day," he said, pressing his fingers deep inside of me.

He pulled his fingers from me, leaving a hollow ache at my core. With his body, he pinned me firmly against the boulder, and as the water gushed around us, he took his lips to mine and entered me with all his fullness. He groaned in my mouth, and gasping for air, I reluctantly untangled from his lips. I trailed his neck with my lips, wanting to feel him. I took his skin between my teeth and squeezed gently before letting go. "I need all of you, Logan," I breathed.

"Fuck, Amber." He gripped my neck, and I clawed him across his shoulders, pulling him so no inch of his skin wasn't touching mine. I wrapped my legs around him as he held me and knocked toe-curling, sweet pleasure into me. "Logan," I said, a coil of tension wound so tight I was about to explode at any moment.

My hands bundled into a fist, knotting them around his neck. Again, he found my parted lips, his kiss laced with desire and thirst. He sucked in more breath as he filled me, harder and deeper. His warm, wet tongue traced my neck down to my swollen nipples. Warmth radiated through me as my sex clenched around him. Everything tensed until finally I surrendered to the euphoria. "Logan!" I breathed, almost dizzy from lack of oxygen. My legs, like jelly, slipped below his hips.

"Sweet fuck!" he yelled as he filled me and slumped his head on my shoulders.

After a few moments, I opened my eyes, my senses returned, pulling me out of my ecstasy. I had gotten lost in his smell, the warmth of his body, his muscles, and the feeling of his arms around my shoulders as if he were protecting me.

He kissed me on the lips, slowly, his mouth like a drug I craved. I loosened my arms around him, then legs, dropping them completely. Eventually, I untangled myself from him.

"You're something else, you know that, Amber?" He pushed a strand of hair behind my ear that had fallen across my face. The ecstasy I'd felt a moment ago was now muddled with confusion.

"I broke my rule. I never break my rules. Ever."

His mouth tipped into a shy smile. His lips stained from my lipstick. "Is that a bad thing?"

"You think I'm crazy, don't you?" I blurted, feeling so out of control, it hurt.

He widened his eyes. "No, I don't."

What have I done?

12

LOGAN

"You know I've realized something," I said.

"What's that?" She pulled the starched sheet over her bare skin. We'd barely gotten back to the cabin before our desperate hands undressed one another and had bone-melting sex like two people reunited after being separated by war for five years. Intensity had clawed at me, and I tried my damndest to please her before I came. And by the skin of my teeth, I did.

"I've realized, regardless of the shit stinky-ass cabin we're in, it's bearable if you're with me."

She blinked, and a blush of crimson spread across her chest. "Thank you."

"Sorry, was that out of line?" I asked, not wanting her to go but sensed she was slipping away again like after the sex at Babinda Boulders.

"We are both seriously past being out of line," she said. Her lips were swollen and cheeks patchy red from my rapid-fire kisses and the stubble on my jaw. "I think you know by now, I'm a bit of a complex cat."

"I can do complex," I said.

Her smile reached her eyes, and it lifted something inside of me to new heights. "Come on. Let's go."

"Where are we going? I'm naked in your bed and in the middle of nowhere!"

"You are, and deliciously so, but all this exercise has given me a serious appetite." I swatted her peachy ass and hopped out of bed in nothing but my birthday suit.

"Oh, me too. When I googled the mine before the trip, I noticed a few restaurants to the south in Dobo Creek."

"Not a good idea, that's where Vincent and Jacob are staying." I pulled my jeans over my semi, tucking it down into my Calvins. *Shit!* Amber wasn't even near me, and I was ready to go another round with her.

"Agreed. It definitely wouldn't look good if it got back to Chadwick and Carlton if we were… you know…"

"No?" I wanted her to spell out what we were exactly to her. Reading her mind had become hazier than waking to an Ibiza sunrise after a night out.

"It's just not a good idea." She hopped out of bed, snaking the stiff sheet around her svelte frame. "Let's just drive and see where we end up." Amber shrugged.

"Say what? Who is this imposter, and what have you done with my Amber?" Haphazardly, I tossed the seat cushions off the lounge and pulled back the curtains, which then sent particles of thick dust sprinkling into the air.

"What are you doing? You're crazy!" She laughed.

"The Amber I know would leave nothing to chance."

"Ah, well, my stomach is suddenly screaming for food, and when I'm hungry, I get *hangry*."

I stepped closer, wrapped my hand around her ass cupping it and pressed her against my body. "Well, shit, we can't have that!"

She giggled, then stepped out of my grasp and through the open door. "Exactly! I'm just going to slide next door and slip something on. She looked over her shoulder, the sun hit her face, and something expanded inside my chest.

True to her word, I heard the door open after only a few minutes.

"You still not ready?" she questioned through the thin bathroom door.

I smudged a strip of wax throughout my hair. "Of course, I'm ready." I shut the mirrored vanity door, careful not to shatter the corner crack into oblivion. Its shabby appearance humored me now, instead of the irritation and disgust I felt when we first arrived.

I slid the door open and drank her in. Her canary yellow dress cinched her slim waist and rounded out to an eye-popping hourglass. "Insert wolf whistle here!"

She placed her fingers into her mouth and whistled. "You mean like that?"

I grinned. The girl could do it all. "Absolutely like that."

She lowered her head and bent her knees to curtsy. "Why, thank you."

"Gorgeous suits you."

"I guess you're used to gorgeous," she said like a tried-and-tested Google search.

Instantly, I stopped and reached out to wrap her hand in mine. "Gorgeous, yes. Brains, no."

A glimmer of a smirk spread onto her full lips as she accepted my hand.

"Let's go, I'm starving. And God knows, we can't leave a hangry lady waiting." Never had I wanted to hold a woman's hand before, but with her hand in mine, it felt like I imagined what home would be like. Until now, connection and intimacy were foreign concepts, but with Amber, it had come as easy as the sun to daybreak.

"Me, hangry? Now, there's a side you certainly don't want to see!"

Together, we walked from the cabin, our arms rubbed against each other. Her skin reflected the evening sunlight, and her hair formed soft waves from being wet earlier.

I brushed a hand through my just-fucked hair as we walked toward the SUV. "Is this *hangry* thing something I should remember about you?"

"Only if you want to." She glanced over at me, and our stares collided.

"There's no doubt. I want to." I opened the car door for her.

Her lips curled into a smile. She nodded. And in the absence of words, I saw something bloom in her eyes. Something that only she and I shared.

The town of Cragers Creek wasn't a long drive. Dusty roads and stretches of undulating land were all that lay between our fly-in-fly-out site and the town. A blink and you miss the town, with a post office, handful of cement houses, and this restaurant that looked as though it hadn't seen a lick of paint in over a decade. Yet, there was a simple charm about this little town in the middle of fuck-hole nowhere. I couldn't quite put my finger on it, but it was something money couldn't buy. In fact, throwing money at developing the town would probably destroy the quaint old thing altogether.

I wondered if before Danker Gold, a similar town had existed, before their large haul trucks and detonators left meteor-size holes in the earth. Did Carlton and Dad even care? I knew the answer like I knew the back of my hand.

* * *

"You liked it then?" Amber asked.

"Well, bowl me over, that was not what I expected." I'd pretty much scraped the plate clean.

She laughed. "No caviar here, and you look as happy as a pig in mud?"

"I am, indeed. I'm right where I ought to be… if only for a few more days." Leaving her to fly back to Perth was slowly draining the blood from my heart like a slow death.

She blinked, clutching her water glass with both hands. "Well, let's enjoy this limited time then." A hush grew over the table as she cast her eyes downward. "So, the steak was that good, huh?"

"Better than good, and it wasn't Japanese Kobe beef. What do they feed the cows out here?"

She giggled, and it reverberated through me like a breeze on a mid-summer morning. I craved more of it, more of her—with her guard down and her heart open.

"I don't know what they feed them, but I concur. My burger hit the spot."

"Did I hit the spot?" I grinned, unable to miss the opportunity.

"Logan!!" She picked up the linen napkin and threw it at me.

I threw my hands in the air. "Too far?"

Her skin turned beetroot red, and her eyes darted from side to side.

"What is it?" I asked, wanting to get inside that brain.

"At the risk of being mortified or increasing your ego, I have to tell you…"

"Oh, I'm definitely intrigued now."

"You're the first to ever give me… you know…" She glanced up, her hazel eyes soft, her face blazing.

"An orgasm?" *No way.*

"Yes."

My jaw nearly hit the table. "No fucking way. How is that even possible?"

She slunk back into the chair, folding her arms across her body. "My rules, I guess."

"Have you ever given a guy a chance so he can stick around and try?"

"No, not until you." She pushed her teeth between her lower lip. "But it's more complicated than that. How about you? You talk about relationships, and there are several pictures with you and a girl from Perth in the papers."

I tilted my head, curious she'd looked me up and even more that she sounded jealous. "I think you're misconstruing those pictures in the tabloids. Celia is a family friend. We had a thing. She wants more, I don't. Her dad and my dad…" I struggled on the word because he was far from ever being a dad, "… they go way back."

The server approached and reached for her pencil tucked between her ear and frizzy hair. "Can I get you both some dessert?"

I clenched my jaw. "Perfect timing."

Amber glared at me. "No dessert but a double espresso for me. Thanks."

"I'd like the tiramisu."

"Marvelous choice, handsome. It just so happens I made it myself." She winked, and I forced a smile. The server must have been in her sixties, wrinkled and hardened like the drought-stricken dirt around us. She had kind eyes and a charisma, but just terrible timing. She hummed to herself as she retreated, throwing her pencil back and sliding it above her ear. She handed the ticket to a man of similar wiry age—most likely her husband.

"Someone has more than one fan."

"Jealous?"

"Oh, absolutely." She bit her lip and glanced out the window.

"Now you've broken them… tell me, why the rules?"

She shifted her body weight in her seat. Although my question may have been skirting on the edge of dangerous, I needed to know.

"Like I said, it's complicated."

"Is it because you've been in love before, and someone really hurt you?"

"I've never been in love."

The server reappeared with a cake and a steaming cup of espresso. *Gold medal to you lady for the fucking worst timing ever.*

Amber stared out the window, her eyes heavy, her shoulders rigid. More than anything, I wanted the carefree girl back, not the one with the weight on her shoulders, who I didn't know how to help.

"I grew up in an abusive household where Dad hit Mom."

Okay, so that wasn't what I expected. "Shit, Amber."

"It's okay. I moved out as soon as I could, leaving before sunrise on my eighteenth birthday. I caught the bus and ended up in Seaview. I only had enough savings for a few nights in a cheap motel."

I leaned in and rested my arms on the table just to feel closer to her. Wanting to reach out and touch her, but knowing she wouldn't want me to, I refrained.

"Luckily, I got a job waiting tables. Then from my grades at school, I was accepted into the scholarship program for law at university."

"I don't think any of this came down to luck, Amber."

She shrugged. "Maybe, maybe not. I haven't stopped working hard ever since. That was five years ago. I don't know why I told you all that. The only people who know about my parents are Jasmine and Lily."

The two women at the restaurant. "Redhead and blondie you were dining with?"

She smiled. "Excellent memory. Jasmine is the redhead. She's going out with Kit Jones and now living in New York."

"Kit Jones from Four Fingers?"

"Yes."

"He's a pretty decent guy."

"You know him?" Her eyebrows pegged into her forehead.

"I don't *know* him. I just met him at a concert in Turin a few years back."

"Gosh, they're not wrong when they say money creates networking opportunities."

"I guess money opens doors."

She sipped on her piping hot espresso.

I took a mouthful of tiramisu, savoring the flavors of mascarpone, coffee, and biscuit. *Damn, this woman could cook.*

"Jasmine and Lily went to school together, and I met them at college. We've been inseparable ever since."

"So, if Jasmine is dating Kit Jones, is Lily dating Ryan Gosling?"

She laughed. "No, she's with her first true love, Blake."

"I bet Ryan Gosling couldn't make you burst like Krakatoa!"

She nearly spat out her coffee. "Next, you'll tell me you have him on speed dial."

"Not exactly, I've been at a party with him, though."

"Shame." She grinned.

"Is it?"

"Could you imagine the kids from that gene pool?"

"I could." I narrowed my eyes. The sticky air returned, and suddenly, the diner felt stuffy. *What is this girl doing to me?*

She tucked her hands behind her elbows. "I'll grab the bill."

Did she want to get away from me?

As though listening to us, the server ripped off her piece of notepad and popped it on the table, directly between the both of us.

"And Santa farts jellybeans," I said, reaching for it.

Quicker than lightning, she reached for the bill, pinching the edge of the paper before I could. But I slapped my hand down on top of hers and rendered her hand still.

She glanced at me, fear or pain in her eyes—I wasn't sure. If paying a bill was that important to her, I removed my hand.

"Okay," I said, holding my hands up. "That's a first for me."

"I bet," she said, signaling the woman to return.

* * *

There was a box on the shared veranda when I pulled the SUV up to the front door of our twin cabins.

"What's that?" I asked as I unclipped my seat belt.

Amber, quiet on the way home, had suddenly come out of her head and looked toward the front door. She hopped out and briskly set off toward the door. "No idea."

I caught up to her when she moved to rip open the cardboard box. "Oh yes, yes, yes! It's my stuff. Laptop, documents..." Like a hungry piranha, she ravaged through the box. "Everything's here." Relief covered her face.

I didn't care. I wanted her all to myself tonight with no work distraction.

"Gosh, I have so much to do. I wonder if we can go in tomorrow. Have you heard anything, Logan?"

"Ah, I don't know. I haven't checked."

"What do you mean? You've still got your phone, at least. Haven't you checked any emails this entire afternoon?"

"No. Enjoying my time with you felt more important than work."

She rolled her eyes. "We have a deal to get through, Logan. Two more days is all we have."

"I know that, Amber." Irritation chipped away at me like a chisel to rock. Was I purely a convenience to her? The giver of orgasms between emails? "We also have our lives to live too, you know." Without looking at her, I shoved my silver key into the door, turned it, and went inside, shutting the door behind me.

She'd definitely numbed it enough for me not to want to be in her company, but I still didn't want this feeling to go away,

For once, sex wasn't enough.

13

AMBER

After the amazing day at the waterfalls yesterday, I'd broken my rules, and although it was magical, it scared the hell out of me. Since then, my emotions have been up and down and all around. After Babinda Boulders and the way we had one another, fear overcame me, but his soothing voice and calm temperament put that fear on ice. Back at the cabin, we fell into each others arms, tangled between the sheets. I'd spent the afternoon with him, just being me, but the second I'd realized my laptop was at my doorstep, I'd clung to it like a life raft.

I'd been thinking about staying the night in his cabin on the drive back from the restaurant. My heart raced, and my skin became clammy, all because of what it would mean if I stayed. But as quick as I found an escape, I'd taken it with both hands. Literally. Straight back to the comfort of one, in my cabin, that suddenly felt lonelier than ever.

Work was my distraction. I responded to emails and completed varying aspects of the deal until shortly after midnight. Yet, as I crawled into bed, the unexpected feeling I'd been trying to push away returned.

This morning he ignored me. Glued to his phone on the drive into the mine he hadn't said much more than hello. Maybe I shouldn't have eye-rolled him yesterday when he'd suggested time spent with me was more important than work.

Across the boardroom table, I'd tried several times to get his attention. There were moments he'd caught me staring, and his eyes darkened, heating the inside of my thighs and everything between.

The deal would soon be ending, which meant Logan would fly back to Perth or some exotic island. And that was the cold, hard truth. He lived in shiny glass houses while I had to hustle to keep a roof over my head. I shuddered at the thought. He wasn't for me. How could he be when I didn't date? It's just lust—something we could sell by the bottle. I sucked in a breath, remembering his herculean arms pressing my body to his as the water splashed between us. My cheeks warmed. *Not here, Amber.* I took a deep, clearing breath and gave my head a slight shake as I gazed up at the small group working diligently around the boardroom table.

Luckily, Vincent and Jacob were too deep in spreadsheets and machinery logs to notice. Leila was traversing in and out of the boardroom as needed, but when she was in here, she'd seemed somewhat in her head.

I took a chance and peered up through my eyelashes at Logan. His eyes fell onto mine, and I watched as they softened around the edges. I rolled my lips into my mouth, and I followed his gaze sink downward to my mouth. He was the best sex I'd ever had, a distraction against the insane work and pressure I was under. *That's all.*

He smiled, and I couldn't help but do the same in return. The others were completely oblivious to anything going on. I had to remind myself where I was.

Discreetly, he tapped on his gold watch, prompting me to check the time on my laptop. It was approaching five, but with yesterday's evacuation order cutting the audit short, we weren't finished yet.

With a subtle movement, I shook my head. He tilted his head and jutted out his lower lip. It wasn't as though I'd robbed him of his toys. Hell, I wanted to wrap things up and crawl back into his arms but—

"We've ascertained the gold royalties, but the equipment audits need completing." Vincent lowered his glasses as he spoke to Logan, who in turn, shifted his focus to him. "Your brother wanted this turned around and sent to him yesterday."

"You've spoken to Carlton?" I watched as Logan's body shifted from relaxed to tense with the mere mention of his brother's name.

Vincent peered over his laptop, "Of course. I've been in contact with him through this whole merger."

"What the fuck for?" Logan snapped.

"Because frankly, you haven't given a damn about this merger and Amber, Jacob, and I have been working to get this across the line."

"You're out of line, Vincent."

"I don't believe I am, Logan."

The two men stared at each other across the table, neither backing down.

"Shall we just stick to the merger, gentlemen?" I asked.

"Good idea," Jacob agreed, neither of us not wanting to be amid a battleground.

"Fine." Vincent leaned back in his chair and crossed his arms. "Well, did you get yesterday's report from the engineer?"

"Yes," Logan said, still clearly agitated.

Vincent leaned forward placing his palms flat against the table. "And? Is there cause for concern with the gas leak?" Vincent squarely looked at Logan.

"The engineer's report gave the all-clear for us to be back. A faulty reading panel of the gas amounts triggered the alarm, effectively detecting gas when it shouldn't have," Logan fired bullets back at Vincent. "It's not happened before. So don't worry, my brother's precious deal can go ahead."

I watched as Logan's jaw twitched, something was amiss.

He stood abruptly, and his chair flew back with enough force it hit the wall behind him. Logan didn't even look at me. Instead, he turned, walking from the boardroom toward the exit.

My focus landed on Vincent. He *was* out of line. Logan had picked up his game since arriving, and Vincent was just stirring the pot.

"Thank God he's gone." Vincent smirked. His partner joined him, spilling into a grin. Like the two slimy snakes they were.

"I think you were unnecessarily rough on him, Vincent."

He lowered his glasses to glare at me. "Do you?"

His intimidation tactic might have worked on his partner, but he certainly wasn't my superior. I tempered his gaze with my own.

"I do. I agree, he's more relaxed about this deal than we are, but that doesn't mean he doesn't care or isn't across it."

His eyes narrowed as deep wrinkles formed around the edges. I stayed firm in my stance with equal parts tenacity and conviction.

"He is more across this than you give him credit for. Trust me on that one. Anyway, don't you need to be on the audit now?" I said, frustrated I felt the urge to stick up for Logan.

"Such a good timekeeper you are, Amber. I guess if this lawyer gig fails, you can always be an executive assistant."

Fuckhead. I wanted to reach across the table and take to his weathered face like a punching bag. Instead, I gripped the base of the chair. He wasn't getting the best of me. "I'll keep that in mind. Now, you best get on your way. We don't want the accounting audit to hold up this deal, especially when the legal team is all over it."

He shot me daggers, then pushed his wire frames up the bridge of his nose. Slamming his laptop shut, he turned to Jacob. "Come on," he snapped.

I didn't give him another look. instead, I refocused my attention on the email I'd been writing when Vincent decided to kick-off on the man who had my body under some kind of spell.

* * *

The chauffeur dropped me off at the cabin, but Logan wasn't there. Since the boardroom spat between him and Vincent, I hadn't seen him. Nor had Leila, after asking about him on my way out. My calls rang out, and after the fifth time, I figured he just didn't want to speak to me. By now, I definitely had the desperado look down pat, but I just needed to make sure he was *okay*.

Outstretched on the floral quilt cover, I typed the last of my emails. Before long, it was after ten and the humid day had tempered to a cool breeze. I pulled on a sweater, wondering where he'd gone. Loneliness crept over me as the cabin took on a different feeling with his absence.

The phone buzzed, and I nearly jumped out of my skin. Frantically, I patted the quilt and hoped it was Logan.

Dammit! I wasn't that lucky.

"Jazzie, hi."

"Hey, gorgeous. How's the deal going?" Her voice was like comfort food.

"Busy."

"And?" she pressed.

"And what?"

"Ah, Lily told me the guy from the restaurant is your boss?

And you failed to mention you already shagged him in the alleyway! Hello!"

"Ah yeah, then there's that."

"What the hell? You've slept with someone you work with!"

I sighed. "And I broke my second rule. I slept with him again." A brief smile crept on my lips.

"Ah! I couldn't be prouder of you."

I laughed. "Jazzie, it's not good. I shouldn't laugh. It is definitely not funny. I don't know what I'm doing. I'm knee-deep in whatever this is, and I can't get out of it."

"Why would you want to get out of it? Aren't you having fun?"

"Yes, I guess. Logan is… well, he is irritating and snobby and—"

"What?"

"Underneath all that, he's… nice. Really nice."

"Nice? I've never heard you talk like this. Tell me, is your work suffering because of him?"

My work? I thought about that for a minute. "No, not at all. It's all going well."

"Well, then, fuck your rules and enjoy it!"

"I guess you're right. But I'm in unfamiliar territory, and it scares me," I whispered.

"I really think you ought to be more scared of small planes with mechanical issues than a man treating you right."

"Good point."

"You're nuts, you know. You're not scared of that, but you are scared of a man and the potential that exists beyond one night?"

"At least I broke a rule or two. It's a start. We can't all be Gandhi, Jazzie."

"Gandhi? Ha! The words Gandhi and sex in an alleyway do not belong in the same sentence."

"I'm going straight to Hell."

"I'll light the fire for both of us, hun."

I laughed. She was so right. *Where was he?* I just wanted to take his pain away and curl up with him. "Anyway, tell me, how's Kit? Is the tour starting soon?"

"Yes, next week. I'm hoping to join him on the East Coast leg but will have to get back for my gallery exhibition in a month."

"Oh Jazzie, look at you. Living the life most of us would dream about. I'm so happy for you."

"Would you stop saying that?"

"It's true. I know past boyfriends hurt you, and…"

"And I took a leap into the unknown, Amber. Maybe it's time you did the same?"

I blew out my cheeks. "I'm okay, honest, I have everything contained. I'm finally hitting my stride with work and have enough money behind me to maybe even start thinking about sending some back home."

"To your mom?"

"Yes, what do you think?"

"I think that sounds amazing, but how will you get it to her without your dad finding out?"

"Just before I left, she set up her own bank account. I took the details down, hoping one day I could free her from him."

"Oh, hun."

Tears pricked at the backs of my eyes. "I just didn't expect it to take five years."

"Amber, stop. Stop the guilt. It's not your fault."

"I know, but…" I sniffled, the air in the room suddenly became denser, "… I shouldn't have left her."

"Like you've said before, you didn't have a choice."

I sucked in a few breaths, gathering myself. "I think this deal may be taking its toll, sorry. Sob story over."

"Don't you dare apologize. I want *that* Amber back. The one from a minute ago. The raw, honest heartfelt Amber without the armor weighing her down. I don't get to see her often enough."

"I'm here. The armor protects me, Jazzie, you know that."

"I get it."

"Jazzie, baby, who are you talking to?" Jazzie muffled the phone, but her giggles were loud and clear.

"Kit, stop it." She squealed. "It's Amber!"

"Hi, Amber!" Kit's voice boomed in the background.

"I hope you take some time off and come visit me on my tour. I know Jazzie would love it."

"Some of us have work, Kit!"

"Well, you know there's a ticket for you whenever you change your mind," he said.

"Thanks!" I said, feeling grateful.

"Well, I have an image in my mind that I'm keen to erase of the two of you, so I'm going to head to bed."

"Miss you already, Amber. Love you."

"Love you, too, Jazzie. Night."

After I hung up, I blinked away the wetness in my eyes. *Why couldn't I have all that and more?* I deserved love, didn't I?

No. You left her there under his fist. You, of all people, don't deserve love.

Without thinking, I picked up my phone and dialed her number. The last time I'd called was a year ago.

My heart leaped into my mouth as it rang. One ring, two… before I could hear anymore, I swiped end to hang up. *I couldn't do it.* She'd see a missed call but wouldn't know it was me calling. To avoid Dad ever finding me, I'd changed my number numerous times since leaving home.

I threw my phone on the other side of the bed.

Wheels crunched on the road as a car came to a stop. *Logan.* I heard a door slam and the jangling of keys, and I leaped up, yanking the front door open. As I did, a car skidded away and Logan swayed, his eyes vacant as he strayed toward me. "Heya, Ambeerrr."

"Logan, where have you been?"

"Out." Barely able to stand, he fell forward, catching himself on the door frame.

"Geez, you're piss drunk.

"You know something, Amber, you're always right. Doesn't that get old?" He waved his finger, the action propelled him further forward and toward me.

"Get in here." I put my arm around his waist and maneuvered his muscular frame inside the doorway. He smelled like a brewery with undertones of sandalwood and cinnamon.

Between the office and now, he'd unbuttoned his shirt down to his chest, his expensive suit still intact.

"Dammit," he groaned, tripping over my shoes before crashing onto the bed.

Knowing he couldn't move, I shut the door and locked it behind us.

I sat near him, and he opened his eyes. Glassy like yesterday's rock pools, he held his hand up to my cheek. "You're just going to leave me like the rest of them." Then he turned his head, his eyes closing from the alcohol-induced haze.

The fortress I'd built up over the years began to crack at the edges as I glimpsed at the pain in his eyes before he fell asleep. I couldn't exactly switch on and off like I'd done so many times before. Before, I could just forget about my one-nighters, but not with Logan. I wanted to shake him, ask him where he'd been, and why he hadn't taken my calls.

But why, when clearly, I wasn't anything to him? But then, why did he fear I'd leave him?

Before climbing into bed next to him, I untied his laces and slipped off his shoes. Sliding next to him, I dragged the quilt up, so it was over both of us and watched his chest rise and fall, then, as if his mouth was a beacon, I kissed him gently. He stirred lightly, then reached out and rested his hand on my arm.

Confused, but strangely calm, I tried to understand the feeling inside. Nothing about it felt strange. We were in this run-down cabin together, and it seemed perfect. Yet it was foreign at the same time.

Warmth cradled my heavy eyelids, then everything faded to black.

14

LOGAN

The paper-thin curtains did little to block the blunt force of the dawn sun. Normally, I would detest such an intrusion, but this morning, it only highlighted the perfection lying beside me. Amber's ruby lips, golden honey-kissed skin, and dark lashes that fanned the tops of her cheeks were even better in person than in my dreams.

Details about last night were very sketchy with a gaping hole after Vincent pissed me off in the boardroom. But I remembered seeing her in the cabin's doorway, her face etched with worry and annoyance at not knowing where I was. No one had ever worried about me. And even though she was angry, it overwhelmed me knowing she cared.

Her warm breath, a velvety blanket, fell lightly on my chest as she lay on her side, her face inches from mine. Warmth tingled at my chest. I don't think I'd ever been happier. She felt like everything a home should feel like. Leaving her would suck the air from my lungs.

The sun turned her hazel eyes greenish around the edges as she slowly opened her them. I stroked her cheek, and she nestled closer to me. Unable to resist, I pressed my lips to her forehead, kissing her gently.

"You made me so angry last night!" she said, without missing a beat.

"And she's back... good morning to you too!" Gently, I kissed her lips. "I'm sorry, I wasn't thinking."

"Mm-hmm," she said, through clenched teeth. "Where did you go?"

"To be honest, I don't remember all that much. Drinking in the middle of nowhere and convincing the barman to remain open. That part I remember, but that's about it." I wrapped my hand around her waist, pulling her into me in my own morning stretch.

"Don't worry me like that again," she said, her eyes scanning mine.

"Yes, boss."

She let go, and her mouth tipped into a slight grin. She pressed her warm thighs into me, whether on purpose or not, I wasn't sure. Regardless, my morning glory lengthened.

I plunged my lips on hers, taking her in. Our tongues searched one another in a deep, longing embrace. Waking up with her was something I could get used to.

"Logan, we have to go to work," she said just inches away from me, but her eyes burned with the same longing I had.

"Shh, that mouth of yours, just once."

She grinned, then her lips landed on mine. Her hands peeling away my shirt before unbuttoning my pants.

"You don't get all the fun," I said, momentarily taking my lips off hers to wriggle out of my suit pants. Next, I clawed down her silk shorts and, instantly, she wrapped her hands around my cock and rubbed me up and down while she wriggled out of her shorts.

"Amber, you're going to make me come like this," I said, feeling her palm me from base to tip.

My cock grew harder with her touch. I needed her now.

"You have me," she breathed, reading my mind.

After she rolled onto her back, she pulled her camisole top over her head, and I took her breast in my mouth. I wanted all of her as she writhed beneath me. I kissed the underside of her breasts, trailing kisses down to her stomach, and gently pressed my fingers into her.

"Baby, you're so wet." I followed my fingers with my tongue, wanting to taste her. I kissed the inside of her thighs, then plunged into her perfect cunt. She let out a deep, throaty groan, and it only made me want to please her more. I circled her clit back and forth, tasting her sweetness.

"Logan" she said, threading my hair with her fingers.

Her legs tensed around my head, and she moaned louder. I peered up, her eyes were shut tight, and her hand fisted the sheets. *Fuck*, she was hot, and she was close. I plunged back into her, deeper and quicker with the length of my tongue, tasting her salty sweetness. Her hips raised as she absorbed all of my mouth. She released her grip on the sheet and gripped my hair to pull me closer to her core.

"Logan!" she moaned, and I felt her quiver around me as she found her release.

Harder than steel, I moved over her and used my knees to spread her wider. Unable to hold back any longer, I entered her in one hard thrust, and sheathed me completely in her tightness. "Ah fuck," I hissed, filling her deeper with each stroke.

In and out I entered her, feeling her warmth, and it made my skin burn for her. She opened her eyes, her hips meeting mine, thrust for thrust as I filled her deeper. Our moans intertwined as our breaths grew short and shallow. Every cell in my body felt alive and hot as hell as our eyes collided.

"Kiss me," she said. I grabbed her hands in mine and positioned them above her head. As I laced our fingers, my lips crashed into hers. Our heavy breathing and the sounds of our connection echoed the small cabin space. I felt myself building as a heated buzz flowed up my legs to my back. She squeezed my hands tighter as she clenched around me and gripped my hips with her legs, pulling me deeper when she found her release. And that was my undoing. "Amber!" I groaned. My balls tightened, and every muscle contracted and released. My jaw went slack, my body felt heavy as I fell into her.

We didn't move as we caught our breaths. A sheen of sweat coated our bodies but neither of us cared as we basked in the afterglow. After few minutes had passed, our breathing returned to normal. I moved to my side and dragged her close, her ass nestled in the curve of my body.

"I'm going to call my mom today."

"Please tell me you weren't just thinking about your mom when I had my tongue and dick between your legs!"

"Ew, no! I called her yesterday but hung up before she could answer. I guess it's been on my mind."

"Why did you do that?"

"I haven't called her in so long. I guess I felt guilty."

I saw the pain in her eyes, and something in my chest moved. Dammit, I think I was falling for this girl.

"You don't have to feel guilty, Amber. You needed to get out of the situation you were in."

"You sound like Jazzie and Lily. They said the same thing, but deep down, I know I should have taken her with me."

"How could you have done that? You said yourself, you just had enough money for a bus, let alone having enough to support you both."

"I don't know…" her voice trailed off, but I could see she was still in her head.

"You can't change the past, Amber." I closed the gap between us and kissed her cheek.

"I know. I'm going to make it right now. I've saved nearly enough to get her out of her situation. If this deal goes smoothly, I can get the bonus they've promised, and then she can leave him, once and for all. I've checked out affordable places in Seaview if she wants to live near me, that is."

"Let me help you, I have money."

"No. No way." She jerked upright in the bed, pushing away her hair that had fallen on her face.

"It was just an offer."

"I know. I'm sorry, but this is something I have to do by myself."

She kissed me on the lips, then barreled out of bed, her hair dusted the edges of her shoulder blades. *Dammit.* Why couldn't she let me help her? Anyone else would have jumped at the offer. But no, not her.

Maybe that's why I was falling for her. I shook my head.

Why would anyone care for you, Logan, not even your family did?

* * *

"Hi, Logan, got a minute?" Jim appeared behind me as I joked with Amber, who wore her brown hair loose instead of pulled back in a knotted bun. It was lunchtime, and all the workers had assembled on the grassy knoll near the onsite cafe.

"Sure, Jim, how are you, mate? Any word on your daughter?" I asked, stepping away from Amber.

Jim opened his mouth but paused before speaking. "Here's the info you wanted."

I took the envelope Jim held. "What's that?"

His bushy eyebrows drew together. "You're kidding, right?"

I stared at him blankly. Then, like a meteor traversing the sky, flashbacks of last night came thick and fast. A need to know about the gas leaks led to a scouring of the employee database, then a phone call to Jim. A meeting in a bar, and he'd spilled details of a long history of safety issues that plagued Danker Gold.

He spilled because he'd had enough of the conditions at the mine. He feared for his life every day he showed up. Each day he worked at the unsafe mine was another day it could take him from his sick daughter. Then who would pay her medical bills?

But without proof, it was all hearsay. And by the looks of it, Jim had delivered.

Quickly, I took the envelope. "We shouldn't do this here," I said, keeping my voice low.

"Sorry. You all right, mate? You sucked back a few scotches last night."

"And boy do I feel it today." I reached for my forehead and rubbed my throbbing temples.

"Well, for your sake, I hope you feel better. And for all our sakes, I hope you can put an end to what's going on here at Danker Gold or the soon to be Magma Gold mine."

I nodded and watched as Jim walked away. His overalls were covered in the earth's dust, his helmet once white, now smeared with oil. I wanted to help him and piss off my brother and father by blowing the lid wide open on this potato factory of corruption.

I rounded the corner, finding a picnic table away from the crowds of people having lunch. I speed-read the two reports Jim had handed me. *Fuck, it was worse than I thought.* Cover-ups and shortcuts were standard issue according to the real engineer's report. Somehow, Jim had gotten his hands on the engineering report—the real engineering report—not the made-up report they'd paid off a firm to assure the miners of a faulty reader.

Unsure of what my own motivations were at this point, I gazed out at the gaping hole in the earth. With this evidence, I could prove to my family I'm worthy of being a Magma, and not the kid they sent away across the world and didn't want to raise. Or I had another option. I could withhold it from them, let the transaction proceed, and let them buy a dud, essentially losing them tens of millions of dollars.

Angry I couldn't see it through even with as much as I wanted to punish them, I slapped the document in front of me. I wouldn't do it. There wasn't a bone in my body that would allow me to. The safety of the workers was at the forefront of my mind. Every day this damn mine continued was another day they put the miners in danger.

I slid my hand into my suit pocket and pulled out my phone. I glanced around to make sure no one was remotely within ear shot. Maybe this was exactly what I needed to make them proud.

One ring later and my brother picked up. "Logan."

"Carlton, I have some news about the deal."

"You've got three minutes before my conference call."

"The gas leak yesterday wasn't the first. There's been two others in the space of two months, and Danker covered their tracks blaming it on faulty meter readings, when, in fact, it's not that at all."

"Okay."

"Did you hear what I said?"

He paused, and for a moment I thought the line went dead. "How did you find out?"

"You knew about this?" I spat.

"Of course, I know about it."

A vein throbbed in my neck. "What the fuck? Why would you even consider buying this time bomb then?"

"Because it's good business. We have an end plan. A ten-year plan that will see us into the stratosphere into the billions, brother. Do the math."

I slapped my hand to my forehead. "Us?"

"Dad and me and *you* if you play your cards right."

"What cards have I left to play?"

"Celia." *Celia?*

"What about her?"

"You are to marry her by Christmas."

Laughter bellowed from my lips, but when he didn't say anything, I knew he wasn't joking. What kind of sick joke was he on about? "I think you've mixed up your pills today, Brother."

"If you want your share of the looming $1.2 billion deal, that's the card you've been dealt. Pretty fucking good one, I might add, especially with how she was all over you at the house last week."

"What has Celia got to do with this?"

"She doesn't. Her dad, Senator Jones, does. The less you know, the better."

"And if I say no?"

He laughed wickedly, his black heart on full display. "You won't. Deep down, you know what's at stake. You'll be cut off, completely. No inheritance. You'll have to get a normal job to survive, and we both know, brother, you'd rather be dead."

"Fuck you. Don't you even care about the gas leaks? Every day the miners work is potentially a day they may not come home to their wives and kids."

"That's a tad dramatic, Logan."

I stilled on the wooden bench as my hands pulled at my hair. Despair washed over me.

"He's silent for once? So, you're telling me, after all the fucking you've done on my dime, all the yachts and penthouses, and you've suddenly grown a conscious?"

"They're putting their lives at risk every day, going into an unstable mine," I said, my voice deathly quiet.

"We are covered. I've made sure of that. And when things fall into place, we will fix the gas emittance, but until then…"

When things fall into place?

"Now your three minutes are up."

The line went dead.

I stared out to the deserted hole, vast and empty, like my own heart.

15

AMBER

Since lunch, Logan has seemed distracted. It was a far cry from this morning when he'd brushed my forehead and mouth with his full lips, woke me with his touch, then gave me not one but two, spine-tingling orgasms. What we had felt normal, and if I were to admit it, nice. Simply uncomplicated and real. Something I'd never allowed myself to have. My rules kept me from seeing the same man twice. And they served me well. But now, I'd actually allowed myself to care for someone else.

Yet, on the drive to the cabins, he remained silent. I'd heard shouting at lunch, and even though I knew it wasn't any of my business, a crazy need to know he was okay plagued me.

I waited until the SUV left and we'd started walking toward the cabin. His head hung low, and his shoulders slumped inward.

"What was that at lunch? The shouting I heard… we all heard."

"It's nothing." He cast his eyes downward.

"It wasn't nothing, Logan." We all heard the muffled yells. I even tried to distract Vincent, Jacob, and Leila so they wouldn't ask questions."

"My brother is a cocksucker." He kicked a rock, sending dust particles flying onto his navy suit.

"Well, surely, that's not news to you? The deal is practically done now, what's the problem?"

He huffed and shook his head. His standard issue arrogance was back like it never left. "Don't be so naïve, Amber."

I stopped at the front door. Irritation leaped up my spine. "Naïve?" I gritted out. "What are you talking about?"

He lifted his head. "The gas leaks have happened before."

"What?" I fidgeted with my skirt.

"I met with Jim the other night, and he blew the lid off it all. The lies and corruption… it looks like it goes way back."

"Okay. Well, now you know." I stood momentarily and assessed the options, but they were straightforward.

"Magma hasn't completed the sale. Why can't you tell Carlton not to buy it?"

"I did. He still wants it."

"Why would Magma want a mine with corruption and safety issues plaguing it? That's an acquisition ripe for disaster."

"Turns out, they will fix them in time, once we've acquired it."

"We've? Since when have you lumped yourself in with your family?"

He shrugged and moved his foot back and forth on the dusty soil. "Since now."

Something squeezed at my chest. "And you're happy with that outcome?"

"I don't know. I guess I have to trust they will fix it. What else can I do?" His voice pleaded.

"And meanwhile, Jim and his colleagues could get blown to dust the longer it takes?"

"Amber… stop." He raked his hand roughly through his hair.

"It's true, isn't it?"

"And what would you have me do? You would jeopardize this deal? Then you won't get your big bonus. The one you need to get your mom out of that shit-hole situation she's in."

My gaze slammed into his. I couldn't believe how easy he was being on himself. "You know what? I've always found a way. If it's not a bonus, it will be something else… at least I won't have deaths on my conscience."

"I guess you got it all figured out then," he said, sarcasm laced his tone.

My heart bruised like the overcast sky. "No, Logan. But the difference is, I know what's right and what's not. I think it's best if you stay in your own cabin tonight."

As I turned to place the key in the keyholder, I waited for his touch to pull me aside and say everything would be okay. But he didn't. He didn't want to spend the night with me. Self-preservation kicked in as my legs carried me over the threshold. I shut it and pressed against the back of the door. *What just happened?*

Kicking off my stilettos, I watched as they plummeted onto the baseboards, marking them with a black smudge. Logan had reverted to the same guy who didn't care, and it threw me off balance. The more I thought about it, the more I didn't understand him. One minute he cared about Jim and his daughter, then the next, he showed zero remorse if the mine blew up tomorrow.

I grabbed my laptop and flicked it on. While I waited for it to load, I untucked my blouse and plonked onto my bed.

When my laptop was done loading, I re-read the contract, trying to make sense of it all. The amendments that had come through from our senior legal team had been done so via Carlton. The email trail clearly showed it. Almost all the clauses were adjusted that specifically related to indemnity. Magma and the directors were out to cover themselves, having full knowledge of an impending catastrophe.

This wasn't right, and I was part of it, part of a deal that could quite literally blow up in my face. I scratched my forehead and tussled with my bun, eventually loosening it.

Did I want this on my conscience? I slammed the laptop shut. Where did my values lie? I got into law to make a difference, but this deal wasn't making a difference. It was dirty business. Purely for profits, it made the rich richer and endangered the lives of workers around them.

A scorching shower was all it would take to clear my mind. I unzipped my skirt and slid it to the floor, then unbuttoned my blouse, not caring where it landed. The scalding water massaged my skin. The more I stood underneath its flow, the more my skin reddened. And the more my conscious grew on me. I felt like a flower being suffocated by weeds. *But what was the alternative? I couldn't just leave, could I?*

Seconded to another legal job, maybe I could ask for that? But then, how would Chadwick ever trust me again? Or I could just leave. Take the savings I'd saved for Mom and live off of that until I found another job. I turned the shower lever off and let the beads of water drip down my body. The more I thought about it, the more I decided calling Chadwick would be the only option.

After quickly changing, I plonked on the bed and called my boss. It was after seven o'clock, but I knew he'd pickup. "Hello, Chadwick."

"Amber, how are you? Nearly done I see from the latest correspondence."

"Yes, on that, but I have an issue."

"Oh?"

"The engineering report I sent you is doctored. The gas

leaks at Danker Gold have happened before and Magma is fully aware of it."

"What do you mean Magma is aware. How do you know that?"

"Logan informed me."

"I see. And knowing the problems, Magma still wishes to go through with the transaction?"

"Yes. Carlton said they will fix it in the future, but nothing is in writing surrounding that. In fact, the issue doesn't even exist according to the fake engineering report. The only clauses I've dealt with are negating any liability. It's all very strange."

Silence rang down the other end of the line. "Hello, Chadwick?"

"I'm here. And you're calling me because you have an issue with this?"

"Yes, absolutely. I don't think I can pull this together, knowing I'll be putting lives at risk."

"Lawyers don't have a conscious, Amber. We just do what we're paid to do."

I swallowed, my jaw set. "I guess I do."

"Hmm. I see." He paused, and my heart beat like a kick drum. "Well, I see you have two choices. You can continue with this acquisition and get your substantial bonus, or you can leave. I hope it's the former."

Fuck, how had it come to this? "But, Chadwick, how can you not care about the miners?"

"There's a line between caring and doing what they employ us to do."

"Tainted is the line you talk about," I said ashamedly.

He blew out a breath into the phone. "It appears like you've made your decision then."

"It seems I have." *Oh, my God, am I really doing this?*

"I always knew your heart would get in the way of this job."

"Maybe you could have given me a heads-up." My chest tightened.

"You have a good heart, kid, and I wish you well. Try Petersons and Wade. They deal with environmental law. Might be right up your alley. I'll write you a reference."

"Thank you. I'd appreciate that."

"I'll ask my secretary to arrange for your return as soon as possible… such a shame."

The phone line went dead.

Immediately, I dialed Lily as I quickly did the math on the time difference and realized it would be before dawn in New York, and Jazzie would likely be sleeping.

"Hey, girl!"

"Lil." My voice cracked, unable to keep my emotions controlled.

"What's wrong? You sound weird."

"I just quit my job."

"You did what? Why on earth would you do that? You've been working crazy hours to work your way up there."

I pinched my forehead. Doubt casted its ugly shadow over my decision.

"The deal isn't what I thought. It's a long story, one I probably shouldn't discuss but it's putting people's lives at risk, and I can't, in good conscience, be a part of it."

"But I don't understand."

"I don't either, to be honest." And that was just it. I didn't understand how it could all be over due to me having morals.

"Are you sure you needed to quit? What about your mother?"

"I should be able to find another job pretty quickly. I feel like my boss has my back. And as for my mom…" I sighed, a tear escaping from my wet eye. "It will just take a little longer to save up, but I'll get there."

"You know you should just call her, Amber."

"I will. I picked up the phone the other day actually but couldn't go through with it."

"She wouldn't care about money. She'd just want to hear from you. She wouldn't blame you for anything."

"You're right," I whispered.

"Oh, Amber, I'm sending you hugs."

"You can give them to me in person, I'll be back probably tomorrow."

"And Logan? What does he say?"

"I'll tell him tomorrow. I'm pretty pissed at him for not taking a stand himself."

"What with?"

"He could have stood up to his family but didn't. He took the easy route, and I can't understand why. He cares, then the next minute he does this…" I let my voice trail off and thought back to how he actually cared about the deal all along, read my emails, and defended me against the initial backlash from Vincent.

"Well, all that sounds really odd. Should you really let this come between you two?"

"I don't think there is an *us*." *Was there ever?*

"You've never broken your rules. That tells me he is something else. And even if you don't want to admit it to yourself, I think you're smitten as a kitten."

Laughter spilled from my lips. "Even if I was smitten as a kitten, he lives in Perth and spends the summers in Europe. I live in Seaview. It would never work." But as I sat here in my cabin, it dawned on me. Tomorrow, would be the last time I'd ever see Logan, and my heart constricted.

"And Kit is an international rock star who lives in New York with Jasmine from Seaview. If they can make it work, I dare say an out-of-work lawyer and an heir to a billionaire dollar fortune can find a middle ground."

"I can't think about that. I have to find work if I want to keep my flat in Seaview."

"Hmm. Just think on it."

"Okay."

"I've gotta jet, hun. I've got a customer wanting to pay for a bunch of flowers."

"Okay, sorry. Go."

"Dinner tomorrow?"

"I'll text you."

"Bye."

I tossed my phone onto the bed. Strangely, an odd relief flooded over me. I pushed onto my back, resting my damp hair on the pillow. I knew my job, and I was proud of that. The deceit wasn't something I could get past, knowing that I'd be part of a deal that wasn't safe and not in the best interest of every man and woman that worked at Danker Gold. Their safety was jeopardized by not committing to fix the gas leaks and worst of all, writing documents that covered Magma from any wrongdoing from pre-existing issues—no, it didn't sit right. My moral compass was skewed when it came to men but not with this.

My thoughts drifted to Lily and what she'd said earlier. Could I really blame Logan for his family's cover-up or was he just a pawn like me—sent to do the dirty work. They said the rich didn't get rich by sticking to the rules. *Why should I put that between us?*

And was there an us? This last week had been a multitude of rule-breaking, mind-blowing sex, new experiences and banter I couldn't get enough of, all while breaking rules I swore I'd never break.

But therein lay the problem. I hadn't been happier.

16

LOGAN

Yesterday, when I'd told Amber about the gas leak, I left out the most important part. The part where Dad and Carlton had conspired against me, and arranged my future with Celia. *Celia!* The on-and-off-again muse that had always been there when I returned to Perth for Christmas and vacations. A pretty convenience, premeditated by two powerful men—my father and hers, Senator Jones. *But was joining two powerful families the end goal?*

As I glared at my reflection, I hardly recognized myself. Suited up, clean-cut, and sharp, I was molding into more of a Magma every day. It was odd to have a purpose. But even with purpose, the idea of putting the welfare of miners at risk felt like a noose tightening around my neck, one controlled by the ever-powerful Magmas.

Amber was right, but then, she didn't know the entire truth. How could she when I'd kept my arranged marriage from her? Marry the senator's daughter and become richer beyond the one percent of the population. With money and political influence, all I had to do was keep my mouth shut and accept Carlton would be true to his word to fix the gas leak.

Then the ultimate play that pieced it altogether—marry a woman I wasn't in love with. Simple. Happens all the time. Right?

Then why did the cabin walls feel like they were closing in on me. I pinched my eyebrows together, but the ache behind my eyes only throbbed more. None of this felt right. And as each minute dragged by and the night sky gave way to the magenta dawn, the more I circled back to Amber. My decision only got harder. I wanted to burst down her door and tell her to forget about her moral compass, but each time I leaped up, I couldn't go through with it.

What options did I really have? Was I really going to shoot into the wind because of a *fling?* I shook off the word. *Amber was no fling.*

On one hand, commit to the plan, never want for anything in life, and hopefully find happiness with Celia. *Fucking doubtful.* On the other, tell my family to go shove it and be cut out of the family fortune and *work?* But then I'd be free to explore things with Amber if she wanted to. Wanted *me.* Therein lies the question. *Did she want to?* We hadn't even mentioned a future beyond the here and now.

* * *

The SUV tires ground against the dry dirt, breaking just outside our front doors. That's it, enough. No more thinking. I grabbed my phone and checked the time. Our driver was earlier than usual, but I was ready for the day. I'd been up since dawn wondering what I'd say to Amber. It still whirled in my head like a windmill.

As I turned the doorknob, I realized I had only one choice. And that was to tell her about Celia.

Amber stood at my door with her arm raised as though she were about to knock. I took her in, wavy chestnut hair rested on her jade-colored t-shirt. Her long legs clad in denim cut-off shorts. My gaze landed on her makeup-free face, her eyes lighter, clearer somehow. The glow of her skin reminded me of sunlight after the rain.

"No bun and black clothing today?" I asked.

"Nope." A smile peeked from the edge of her mouth.

"To say I missed you last night is the understatement of the century." And that was the truth. I felt lonelier than I ever had before. I was accustomed to the feeling, but this somehow felt different.

"Did you? Maybe I did a bit as well." She looked down to her tan sandals. "I should probably tell you that I quit and can no longer represent Chadwick Lane in the deal of Danker and Magma Gold."

"What, why?"

"I can't work on this deal knowing the risks it poses to workers." She twisted the ends of her hair.

"But quitting… that's extreme."

"Kind of just happened. I guess this is my ride to the airport." She gestured over her shoulder to the waiting SUV, the one I thought was our ride to the mine.

She stared at her feet again, and the innate urge to kiss her overtook me. The inescapable fear that I'd never see her again shook me to the core. I reached for her hand, but she didn't move to take mine.

"Amber. Don't go, this can't be it."

Her gaze moved from her feet to my face. Her eyes were wide and vulnerable. Her mouth parted as though to speak, but nothing came out. She took a deep breath as if to try and start over.

"Come to Perth with me." *There, I said it, and it felt absolutely right.* There was nothing I wanted more than to be around her day in and day out. Her eyes flickered with a lightness I'd come to adore, and in that moment, I knew she felt it all.

Everything we had wasn't some worthless fling. *Dammit, it was real.*

"What the hell is this place? An unmistakable shrill voice sunk me into an undeniable reality. "Where am I?"

What the fuck is she doing here? If murder was legal, I would string Carlton up the nearest eucalyptus tree. I didn't know what was worse—Celia's abrasive voice or her heavily made-up face and three sizes too small striped minidress she attempted to pull down as she maneuvered out of the SUV.

"Who's that?" Amber ping-ponged from Celia then to me.

I stood rooted to the chipped pavers, finding momentary comfort in my shitty cabin.

"Logan!! Oh, thank God."

Celia, what are you doing here?" I couldn't believe this was happening. There was no logical reason for her to be here.

Before I realized what she was doing, her limp hands slung around my neck, and her plastic lips pushed hard against mine. A second was all it took to register what was happening, but it was a second too late. I pulled away and stared at Amber.

Red traced her cheeks, burning the tips of her ears. She said nothing as she bent down to pick up her bags.

"Amber, wait."

"I thought you missed me, Logan." I removed Celia's manicured hands clawing around my neck. She narrowed her eyes, then glared at Amber. "Who's your friend?"

"Amber. And I'm not his friend. We work together or used to." Her voice was sharp like a Samurai sword. I scanned her face, trying to make sense of what she was feeling, but even her staunch pose faltered when she cleared her throat.

"Oh, well, I guess Amber won't get an invitation to the wedding then?"

Her eyes widened. "You're engaged?"

"No! And hang on, Celia. I haven't even asked you. Aren't you jumping the gun?"

"Oh please, they're just little details. We both know this is going to happen."

"Wow," Amber mouthed.

The chauffeur walked toward us. "Amber, the car is ready to take you to the airport."

"Great. *Perfect.*" As she fumbled with her bags she said, "Well, good luck to you both." She turned her back, but momentarily, her gaze found mine. Etched in pain, but shrouded by steel, she had built her protective wall again, and it was like a piano had hit me head on.

"Logan, we are not staying here," Celia said, ignoring our exchange as she brushed past me into the cabin.

I focused on Amber, but she was already walking toward the SUV. I reached for her arm, and she turned around. "Tell me, why did you quit?"

She swatted her hair away from her face. "You're kidding, aren't you? That's what you have to say after that?" Her gaze burned into the cabin behind me.

Behind me, I heard Celia had closed the bathroom door at the back of the cabin.

"I. Uh. It's a complicated situation with Celia. I didn't know she was coming here."

"And so what, I'm meant to care?"

"You care. I can see you care."

Her cheeks flushed. "It doesn't matter, Logan. You're getting married, and I'm out of a job."

"What about your mom, you won't get the bonus."

She exhaled. "It's really none of your business. Any of it. We have nothing to do with each other anymore." She stepped out of my grasp, but I followed her to the doorway of the SUV.

"Stop. Please. It's not what you think with Celia. My father and Senator Jones arranged the marriage. I found out yesterday. I don't love her. I…" I paused.

"Then why the hell are you with her?"

"Like I said… it's complicated."

"Everything is with you. Is it easier for you and more convenient to live a lie?"

"How about you? You're so caught up in your precious career, so you don't have to think about your own life. You live by your rules, not bothering to open yourself up to even the possibility of finding love."

She blinked rapidly, her cheeks turning magenta. "At least I have a career, one I've worked my ass off to get. You're just living off Mommy and Daddy and taking nothing by the horns because you can't handle any kind of responsibility!"

"I can't help that I have the Magma name!"

"Don't do that. Don't blame your lack of caring or responsibility on money."

"Easy for you to say when you have little to lose. I have everything to lose!" I exclaimed.

"I may not have zeros in my bank account, but I have something you will never have. I have purpose, and I have values. You can do so much good with your wealth instead of partying and pretending you don't have a brain. Instead, why don't you stand up for what is right? Deep down, I know you want more. If you think you have everything, think again."

"Why should I even try when they think I'm a failure anyway? No one has ever cared enough to expect anything of me. It only matters to them if I marry Celia."

"And what matters to you, Logan?" She stepped into the car, and I propelled my body forward, preventing her from shutting the door.

"This isn't about Celia or the deal. This is about you and me."

"There is no you and me, Logan. I used you, and you used me. Surely, you should be used to that by now."

I let go of her hand. Her words hit me like a Mac truck.

She blinked rapidly, then quickly focused her attention forward.

I moved away, away from Amber, away from the idea she was my perfect match.

"Maybe. But for once, you let your wall down. You broke your own rules… and maybe, just maybe, you let the best thing in your life go."

Momentarily, she glanced at me, then looked away but not before I noticed the whites of her eyes gloss over.

"Loges, darling…" Celia's machete voice cut through silence.

Any softness Amber had left in her eyes, hardened to stone. "Goodbye, Logan." Then she pulled the door closed and effectively cut me off.

The car skidded against the red earth, leaving a plume of dust in its wake. Terracotta earth dusted my navy suit, and I stood frozen as the shower of memories fell over me one last time.

17

AMBER

My mouth was drier than the Sahara, and the throbbing in my head was louder than an overzealous fan at a football stadium. I rolled my body up off the lounge and let out a groan. Spilled cereal boxes, red-stained wine glasses, and strewn clothes replaced my usual orderly apartment.

What day was it? The days had blurred into one since returning from Danker Gold about a week ago. My apartment had been my refuge. The shades were drawn, but it wasn't evening. The apartment took on a musty scent as though fresh air hadn't occupied the space in some time.

I clutched my stomach as a cramp hit me. What did I expect, living on a diet of red wine, preservative-filled crackers, and Cheerios?

Somehow, in the space of two weeks, my career high and promise of a bonus had been ripped out from under me because of my own values and sense of responsibility. I'd failed to help Mom get out of her abusive situation and delayed it for the unforeseeable future, and if I didn't find myself a job soon, I'd be crashing at Lily and Blake's.

All of that mattered, but not nearly enough as the sting I felt when I found out about Logan's engagement.

I picked the lint off my black leggings and stared at the half-empty bottle of shiraz on the coffee table. Alcohol, the sedative it was, had numbed the pain. But drinking in the morning wasn't something I could master, even in my hazed state. I threw the bottle into the bin and caught its residual vinegary whiff. My stomach lurched into my throat, and quickly I leaped up, my legs heavy like unoiled machinery. Somehow, I made it to the bathroom, dry-wretched but purged nothing.

I really should try to eat something. I leaned up against the cold tiles and snaked down the wall. *Get it together, Amber.*

Loud knocking pulled me away from my self-loathing. Like earlier in the week, I ignored it. I closed my eyes, resting the back of my head against the tiles. My mind drifted to a better time. but the thudding didn't let up. *Bang! Bang! Bang!* This time louder and accompanied by a familiar voice. "Amber, I know you're in there. Now open up before I kick the goddamn door down."

Fuck! Knowing Lily, she wouldn't go away until she saw me alive. Slowly, I pulled myself up off the tiles.

"Get your ass up and open the damn door," she yelled into the hollow-core door.

"I'm coming." Groaning with every step, I swung open the door. Lily stood hands on hips and as cross as a rattlesnake.

"Geez, death looks better than you."

"Nice to see you, too, Lil."

I left the door open and walked toward the lounge.

The door closed, then I heard a disjointed move, breaking the sound of her footsteps behind me. "Look at this place… I can't walk in without tripping over something!"

"Make yourself at home," I said, flopping onto the armchair.

"What the hell is going on? You don't pick up any calls. I've left messages, Amber."

Purposely letting myself wallow in self-loathing and pity was easy when disconnecting from the world. And I did that the second I'd returned to Seaview by switching off my phone.

"My phone died."

"Have you heard of a charger?" she countered, not buying it for a second.

I shrugged.

"When you told me you'd quit, you seemed relieved. I thought you were okay with your decision?"

"I am. I could no longer represent Chadwick Lane in the deal."

"Then what's up? This display..." she gestured her arm around the bombsite that was my apartment, "... this is definitely not the poised and in-control Amber I know. Is it your mom or is it Logan?"

Lily sat on the velvet lounge beside me and placed her hand on my knee. I peered up at her, then let my head slump as I focused vacantly on the floor.

"I know you'll get another job, and I know you know that. So why the wallowing? Why shut out the world?"

I exhaled loudly.

"Is it your mom?"

"She's part of it."

"So Jasmine was right."

"Jasmine?"

"Yes, you know your other bestie in New York, who's also been trying to contact you day and night?"

I rolled my eyes.

"She thinks this is about Logan, and so do I."

My shoulders lifted as I sucked in a breath.

"And we're right," Lily said. "Just saying his name, your face went from gray to subtle rose."

I shook my head. "He just said some things that were so real. You know?"

"Like what?"

"I'm guarded, and I don't open up to the possibility of finding love."

"He's spot on there. You designed the rules you keep for that reason."

"They've kept me safe and in control, Lily." My voice croaked as my eyes prickled with tears.

Lily jumped up and moved to sit beside me. She pulled me close and embraced me in a firm bear hug. "They don't serve you anymore. Did you ever think that maybe you relaxed your rules around Logan because you felt something with him you've never allowed yourself to feel before? He was different to all the other men, and deep down, you needed to explore that."

I wiped away the wetness on the tops of my cheeks. "It doesn't matter, though. He is getting married."

"What? Since when is he engaged?" Lil's voice thundered. "What the hell kind of show is he running here?"

"Well, he's technically not engaged, but it is imminent. It's all arranged."

"Arranged? Sounds more like deranged to me. Well, he obviously doesn't love her if it's arranged."

"Her name is Celia Jones from Perth." The chauffeur had divulged an earful about Celia on the way to the airport. To say he didn't want her in the car again was an understatement. Moaning about everything from the brand of champagne to the comfort level of the leather seats—she sounded like an entitled ass-licker.

"Senator Jones' daughter?" Lily asked.

"What Senator?"

"Jim Jones, the senator for Lands and Environment."

I chewed the inside of my cheek. "Ah, how do you know this?"

"For someone brighter than a star, you astound me sometimes, Amber. My friend from the floristry course. Caroline is an activist. She's been telling me all about lobbying the states and territories for less deforestation. She also mentioned the senator she is lobbying to… one Senator Jim Jones."

"Right… and?"

"Anyway, dearest fat lips, Celia appears in the society pages more than McDonald's churns out Big Macs."

"Well, that doesn't change a thing. She probably lives in a perfect glass house with her perfect hair and perfect life. Just the kind of *perfect* Logan needs."

She shook her head. "I feel like getting a BB gun and stinging you right where it hurts. Are you listening to yourself? It's a marriage of convenience, not of love. Do you love him, Amber?"

"I don't know what that is." The response rolled off my tongue quicker than the feeling that started squeezing at my chest.

"It's when you want to slap them and kiss them at the same time. It's when you're apart, you can't stop thinking about him. It's deep in the pit of your stomach, where things make little sense, but everything seems right where it should be."

I rubbed my temples. "I don't know, Lily. I just don't know."

"Let go of your guilt, then you can be free to think and feel."

"What are you talking about?"

She got up and walked over toward the round table. Clutching my phone in her hand, she held down the button to switch it on.

"What are you doing?"

"You need to call your mother. Well, what do you know, your phone is not dead?"

"I know."

"You know you need to call your mother, or you knew your phone wasn't dead?"

I frowned. "Both."

"I'm here. Go, I'll wait."

"Now?" I asked, knowing the answer to my question.

"If not now, when?"

She had a point. I stared at her unwavering eyes. I knew she was right. All the guilt I'd carried for leaving Mom after turning eighteen, then only speaking to her a handful of times was shameful. And the guilt had stuck with me like the plague.

It wasn't my fault she was in her situation. I just had the motivation, skill, or whatever else you want to call it to get out. She just wasn't so lucky.

Messages came in rampant and fast as my phone beeped to life.

"Well, well. Three messages are mine, but the rest? For someone without a job and a boyfriend who is presumably engaged… you certainly are popular." She raised her naturally bushy eyebrows. "I'm going to clean up this mess before the rodents start nesting here and you have a plague on your hands. Now, go call her."

"Okay." Slowly, I got up from the lounge, my phone in hand as I wandered into my bedroom. It, too, had seen the saber from *Star Wars*, a war zone of mega proportions. I couldn't even remember how or when I'd destroyed it.

Before I could think things through a million times, then another million, I pressed on her name, and after a few rings, her familiar warm voice echoed down the phone.

"Hello?"

My heart thundered and rendered me speechless.

"Amber, is that you?"

I paused, then exhaled. "Yes."

"Amber, I'm so pleased it's you. How are you? I've missed you so much."

Instead of resenting me, she'd missed me?

"I'm okay, Mom. How are *you*?" I emphasized the word *you*. An educated woman, she knew exactly what I meant.

"Same as when you left, but that's all in the past."

"How's that?"

"Hang on," she whispered. In the background, I heard footsteps. It sounded like she was taking stairs… then a creak. *Was that a door closing?*

"Mom?"

"I'm here, just had to make sure he wasn't listening."

"Doesn't sound like anything is in the past."

"It is, my dear. It is. A beautiful woman called me up a few days ago, telling me I'd won an apartment in Hastings. Can you believe it?"

"What? Are you serious?"

"Yes, I could scream. I'm so excited! You know I don't even remember entering the competition!"

"Mom, are you sure it's not a scam phone call where they want your credit card details?"

"I did at first, and I was very cautious. But everything is legitimate. She's sending the deed tomorrow. I move in next week!"

"What? Oh my God, that is unbelievable! Hastings is the suburb next to me. It's only ten minutes away."

"I don't even know where you are, Amber." Her excitement wavered.

"Seaview, Mom. I'm so happy for you." Tears started escaping down my cheeks. "I'm sorry I wasn't the one to help you financially. I really tried. I'd save a good portion of my paycheck each week, hoping to give it to you, to set you free. The last chunk was a bonus that fell through…"

"Amber, sweetheart, it's never been your responsibility to free me from your father."

"But it has, Mom." I wiped the floods of tears rolling down my cheeks.

"Oh, Amber. The day you left was the day I knew in my heart my little girl was being brave, making a decision I couldn't. You had the courage to leave. You shouldn't have given it one thought, let alone save your paychecks for me. I'm the one who should apologize, letting you grow up in a household of dysfunction and evil."

"Mom, I don't know how you did it all those years." My legs felt like lead as soft sobs escaped my body. Five years of built-up tension and guilt were finally purging from my body. The heavy burden I carried was no longer mine to carry.

"Listen carefully, Amber. You need to let go of all of it. I'm okay. I'm making my move now… we can be together… he can't harm me anymore. He can't harm us."

I sat on the floor against my bed. "But what if he finds you?"

"He won't try. He's been having an affair for years. Plus, now he's too frail. The only reason I couldn't move out sooner was because I was broke, but now, with this apartment, I can."

"Oh, Mom."

"*You* okay?" she asked. Her honey voice, still like I remembered.

I exhaled. "Yes, I still can't believe you won an apartment."

Logan wouldn't have done this, would he? The thought left as quickly as it came. *As if.*

"I know, me neither. I feel like it's too good to be true!"

Too good to be true? "Can you send me the email correspondence you received?"

"Yes, of course, but I know it's legitimate. I'm just so happy you called, dear. I wanted to call you so many times but didn't know how to reach you."

"I'd love to see you, Mom."

"I'd like that so much too."

"Call me when you arrive in Hastings, and I'll help you get set up."

"I'd like that, sweetheart."

"Love you, Mom."

"Love you to the moon and stars and back again. Never forget that, Amber." The last time she'd said that was the night I left home.

"I won't."

18

LOGAN

Over the course of the last week, a torturous reel played through my mind. Every minute without Amber was a lashing to the heart, a deep unrepairable wound. Never mind Celia's abrupt timing or Carlton's stinging betrayal of the highest order. Funnily enough, the fog had lifted, and I realized Amber had been completely right this entire time.

She'd seen me, truly known me, and wanted me just as I am. Not a Magma brother with riches beyond measure but plain old me. Denying ourselves the pure carnal attraction we had was sinful. It went against human nature and the very fabric of the term *fate*.

Damn, I didn't know we'd end up working together. Worse still, I didn't think she would be the one to make me believe in myself, believe I'm not just a title and an heir, a meaningless pawn in my family's wealth. She didn't see me as a stepping-stone like so many other women had. She had nothing and risked it all for the sake of her values and morals. I'd met no one like her, and I missed her more than I ever thought possible.

I'd arrived back in Perth less than three hours ago and had it all together. Nerves were completely absent, which, considering what I was about to do, was odd. But I guess when you feel you've already lost it all, you've got nothing to lose.

I pulled up to my parents' fortress of a house. Oversized gates with gold spear tips opened to the limestone paved driveway. The latest facial recognition software had made intercoms a thing of the past and allowed me to enter without speaking to a soul.

Obscene and modern, it screamed I'*m richer than Warren Buffett*. Perched on the cliff side, the house was all glass and metal. It felt hollower than a termite-infested log. The house lacked soul and love. Perfect for magazine covers—which they regularly featured in—but not a home where I'd ever felt comfortable. The constant competing with Carlton, the parental neglect that led to my attention-seeking behavior were all the memories I had. Then there were the nannies and nannies tasked to be my stand-in parents.

I glided my Aston Martin DB9 into the parking spot and closed the car door, looking around one last time at the house. Rolling green lawns bled into sandstone flower beds that spilled with bright yellows and soft pinks. Flowering plants were rare in this harsh climate, but you wouldn't even know it here. It had the feel of an English garden, yet we were in the midst of a drought. Money can truly buy you anything, even a foreign garden.

But that wasn't me. I didn't need to stand by any of that. It all made sense now, and the golden carrot they'd dangled in front of me could go to Hell.

"Logan! Aren't you a strapping man!" Gertrude, the housekeeper, was still the same as I remembered, with her friendly smile and warm heart. But over the past decade, her bright eyes seemed faded as wrinkles creviced the corners of her eyes. She pulled me into a tight hug, and I willingly embraced her.

"Gertrude, so nice to see you," I said, remembering how she stuck up for me time and time again when everyone else seemed to defend my brother.

"Oh, how I miss you, Logan! I was on leave when you came back a few weeks ago."

"How is Timothy doing, Gertrude?"

I remember as kids playing with her son, Tim. When she couldn't find a sitter, she'd hide him in my room so I could have a play buddy. We'd play for hours and hours, and I realized what a genuine friend Tim was. When Mom found out I'd been cohorting with the *help* as she put it, she'd threatened to fire Gertrude if it happened again.

"He is perfect. He is set to wed his fiancé, Finegan, this summer. I hadn't told him you were back because I didn't know how long you'd stay in Australia."

"You can tell him I'm back for good."

She smiled, and the dimple in her cheek lifted. "Well, mark the date on your calendar. December first for the wedding."

"Absolutely, I'll be there. Can you put me down for a plus one?"

She raised her eyebrow, and I smiled. "Sure can. Now best get your tushy in the dining room before I get in trouble!"

"Yes, ma'am!"

She pinched my cheeks, an endearing thing she did when I was a kid, and I felt sorry for her since she was still working in the castle of leeches.

"Darling, so nice you could join us," Mother said, only bothering to glance away from her magazine enough to regard me from head to toe. "You look terrible."

"Mother, a pleasure as always." I walked around the marble-slabbed table and leaned in, giving her a one-sided kiss. It had always been that way. Spoiling her perfect makeup with a kiss was out of the question. Since I was young, she'd said,

"One must always appear primed and perfect." Maybe that's why air kisses were invented.

Two weeks ago, she hadn't been this stretched and toned, had she?

Dad perched himself at the head of the ridiculously long rectangular table—the size the queen would have to host her stately dinners. His glasses perched on the bridge of his nose, thinning silver hair and weathered face, his once fit frame now spindly and emaciated, finally showing the fragility of the man who I'd hardly known all my life.

"Logan," he said, not bothering to look up from the documents laid out between him and Carlton.

"Father." Fuck, it pained me calling him that. But when I'd come back that first year after being sent to England, I called him by his first name, Charles, and was slapped across the face. Never did I try that again after that.

"Carlton." My brother, engrossed in documents, didn't move.

"Why haven't you sent the final audit and agreements through from Danker Gold?" Dad asked.

"I can see where Carlton gets his bedside manner from."

He glared at me. At least I'd got his attention. "I'm not to be trifled with tonight, *boy*."

Call me boy, one more fucking time. The vein in my neck throbbed, and I exhaled as I reached for the crystal tumbler and liquid ale.

"Ah, corporate life is too tough for you then, rather spend your days on my yachts in Sardinia?" Dad grinned like he'd won some kind of bet.

"Not at all."

"Perfect. So, Carlton tells me you're going ahead and marrying Celia in December."

I sat down and lifted my legs, crossing them atop their precious table.

"You know what… I wondered why you were both so keen on me coming back and marrying Celia."

"She is perfect for you, darling." My mother glanced over her magazine. A look of horror flashed on her face when she saw my expensive Italian loafers resting on her perfect marble tabletop.

"What are you doing?" Carlton sneered through his porcelain veneers.

"Oh, are my feet an imposition?"

Dad sneered. Carlton placed his hand on Dad's forearm. "What are you playing at, Logan?"

I took my feet off the table. Now I'd gotten all their attention, it was time to slay like my life depended on it.

I pulled a piece of paper from inside of my sports jacket and slid it across the table toward Dad.

"This is the apartment you will buy in Hastings."

My brother laughed, not even bothering to look at it.

I continued unperturbed and pulled another piece of paper but left it folded. "And, as soon as this deal is finalized in sixty days, you will have one month to fix the gas leaks."

Dad laughed, his voice throaty from all the late-night cigar and scotch sessions in the retreat room with his golfing buddies.

Opposite me, I glanced at Mom. For once, I could see she felt something—fear and confusion traced her face.

My face remained deadpanned, but inside, my heart pounded faster than a Bugatti.

"You're fucking off your rocker if you think I'm agreeing to that," Carlton said, pushing out his chair.

"I'm not asking you, I am asking Mother and Father who, if I'm not mistaken, are the majority shareholders of Magma."

Mom widened her eyes.

"No," Dad's voice roared. "You think you can come in and tell me how to run my shop? I knew we sent you away for a reason. You were never the brains. You were always trouble."

"You invested all your time into Carlton, completely ignoring me. He could do no wrong in your eyes, and I was pitted as the troublemaker from the get-go. I never had a chance. All I ever wanted was parents who loved me, but you couldn't even do that. You gave it all to him."

"Oh, Logan. Your father thought educating you in the finest overseas schools would be the best thing for you. Your behavior, well, it was…" Mom tilted her head.

"Everything I did was to get your attention, and that included the fire in the west wing. Can you really blame a kid for trying to get his parents' affection?"

Relief flooded me. I'd said my peace, and the outcome didn't matter.

"Poor Logan, feeling left out, brother?"

"We might be cut from the same cloth, brother, but we are absolutely nothing alike."

"Why are you really here, Logan?" Dad asked, placing his palms flat on the table.

"I know why you dragged me back here. You wanted me to learn the family business, but you had no intention of really letting me learn from you. You never had given me the time of day growing up, so why did I think you would now, all these years later?"

"Oh, Logan, it wasn't like—" I put my hand up, silencing Mom and her fake tears.

"So, I got digging. And you know what I found? Money trails. Large donations from Magma to a certain senator. Going on for *years*. Then, I wondered why Magma had donated just over a million dollars to Celia's father, Senator Jones. It turns out our good ol' politician, who swore to serve the people, is in the middle of selling crown land. Land, that is next to Danker Gold, the mine Magma is in the middle of acquiring. Potentially tripling its output and turning the once lackluster, trouble-filled mine into a fortune of gigantic proportions."

"How do you know this?" Carlton snapped.

Ignoring him, I continued. My Bugatti heart disappearing. "So, then I thought, what has Celia got to do with it? She doesn't love me. Wanting me back home under the guise of working for the family business was clever. You knew I'd fall for that because I've only ever wanted to be a part of this family. But orchestrating a marriage with the Senator's daughter… perfect. She gets to marry into Australia's richest family, and Magma will gain the gold-filled land Senator Jones is conveniently offloading. Magma gets richer beyond measure."

"No!" Mom gasped, taking her perfectly manicured hands to her mouth. Either she was a brilliant actress, or she didn't know about this scheme at all. *Did that mean she actually wanted me back home?*

"There's one hitch. You thought you could buy me off, just like everyone else. But I'm not like everyone else. I'm not like *you*, Dad."

His nostrils flared. "Well played, son. Well played."

"I'll repeat myself. Purchase the apartment by the weekend and fix the gas leaks within thirty days of acquiring Danker Gold, and I might keep my mouth shut about the senator and his grubby payments. Oh, and forget Celia. Jesus, I'd rather marry a wet rag."

"What proof do you have?" Carlton snapped.

"So, it's true, Charles?" Mom stared at her husband who ignored her.

"Paper trails, bank transfers…" I started pulling documents from my pockets.

Dad held up his hand. "Enough. Why are you doing this? You know we'll just cut you out."

"Please do. I don't want you to hold money over me again. I have values. Values I never thought I'd find, least of all in the middle of a deal working for Magma."

"It's that woman, isn't it? The lawyer. I heard she quit over the fucking gas leaks too. Well, fuck you, Logan, and fuck her. I've spent three years on this deal and to think you can just tear it up overnight? You're fucking out. Out!" Carlton yelled.

I exhaled and pushed my seat out. "Fine by me."

"If I don't see the deed to that house by morning, I'm going to the media, and you will all be done. You can exchange this shiny house for metal bars."

"Logan, wait." Mom rounded the table quicker than I'd ever seen her move. "I'm sorry, I didn't know any of this."

"Well, maybe you should have, Mom. You *are* half of this company. Maybe realize how profits are prioritized over miners. Miners like Jim, whose daughter is terminally ill. He is slaving away at the mine just so he can pay his daughter's medical bills."

"Jules, sit down," Dad said.

"No, Charles, you've treated our son like this all these years, driven him out and now this? You don't get to tell me to sit down."

That's new. That's the first time I'd ever heard her speak to Dad like that. If it shocked him, he hardly showed it, giving his attention to Carlton, whose voice cut low. Mom placed her shoulder on mine. The most comfort I can remember her ever giving me.

"Mom, I don't give a fuck if you disown me, you've done that before. And the money, well, we all know that doesn't buy happiness. Exhibit A, right here," I said, staring down both of the males in my life. "So, cut me out. I really don't care anymore."

"I'm sorry, I knew none of this, I promise you. I wouldn't have let them go ahead with Celia, this deal, the whole bit. Believe me, please?" It sounded like a desperate plea.

I didn't know if I should believe her or not, but all my life she'd been out of the business, aloof, only focusing on her social circles and mingling with the people who adored her. But now this blonde woman, whose eyes gleamed with water, appeared to be the most honest and raw with her emotion, I didn't know who she was.

"Sure, Mom."

"I'll make this right, Logan. I promise you."

Nothing would ever be right with Dad and Carlton. With them, I was done.

19

AMBER

While I waited for Mom to send through the email correspondence, I returned to my shit show of an apartment. Lily had cleaned what she could before returning home to make a surprise dinner for Blake's birthday. After my phone call with Mom, I needed time to clear my head. I'd ushered Lily out the door as quickly as I could.

It had seemed premature to mention the apartment to Lily without knowing for sure if she'd won it from a competition or if it was from Logan. *No.* I still fought with myself thinking he'd done anything like that, but from the corners of my body, hope stemmed like a four-leaf clover.

I collapsed on my bed, exhausted after a mammoth cleaning effort. As the sea breeze kissed my skin, I felt a chill, so I pulled up the quilt and closed my eyes. My mind drifted to his dark eyes, silken hair, and full lips. A lonesome tear pooled in the corner of my eye. I regretted saying I used him as I sat in the SUV. It wasn't true, but self-preservation was a motherfucker and, by saying that, I knew it would push him away for good.

Why then, did the cut of his body and the shape of his face shadow me? I couldn't forget his touch, his kiss, and his true heart. But Celia had her claws in her prey and soon their picture-perfect faces would splash across the society pages. I didn't have a choice but to forget him, forget us, and move on. Whatever I had with Logan would never measure up to marrying the senator's daughter. Then there's the crux of it. I'd never have the guts to tear my own walls down and welcome love into my life. My rules gripped me like a straitjacket—to keep me safe and protect me from ever feeling.

* * *

In the morning, I'd stacked the refrigerator with food that was mostly on sale from the grocery store. Then I went for a stroll down Seaview Beach. The salty air and smell of seaweed did nothing to keep my mind at rest. If I wanted to keep stocking my fridge with food, I needed to start job hunting.

Checking my phone was an addiction. First thing in the morning and last thing at night, checking emails was like breathing air. Work and life meshed into one with no clear boundary, and just maybe it had become all too consuming—a distraction from the actual truth—the one Logan had rightly uncovered, and I hadn't even realized. Work served as a distraction to my own feelings. The need for self-resilience after living with a father who shrank my mother into a box was always near the surface. An independent spirit who, over the years, had lost her spark. Something I was determined to avoid. I'd stepped into my own gilded cage with my craving for independence. Locking myself from any type of feelings and creating my set of rules, making relationships impossible. The net result—a workaholic with no social life and zero chances of ever falling in love.

It seemed strange that I'd only been out of work for a

week, and the pattern of stepping back from devices came more easily than I thought. But as I waited for my double espresso to lose steam, I decided it was time to check emails and catch up with the world that lived beyond my week of self-pity and loathing.

As my emails loaded on my laptop, I sighed. No, I don't want two quilts for the price of one, nor do I want the latest vacuum or a Russian bride. *Delete, delete, delete.* I clicked on an email from my old boss.

Amber,

I spoke with Rachel Dawson over at Crighton's law firm, and she's keen to get you in for an interview. I suggest you take her call because you haven't returned mine.

Regards, Chadwick
Partner, Chadwick Lane

Oh! That would be amazing. *Shit!* I hadn't listened to any messages since being back. *What if she'd called?*

Quickly, I scanned the other eighty-six emails. Spam and more spam. Mom hadn't emailed the correspondence from the apartment win, but I guess she was busy packing.

Nothing from Logan. *Zilch.* Why would there be? As I wandered through the last of the emails, it struck me. He hadn't tried to reach out, hadn't emailed, and he wouldn't have called. Sadness washed over me.

I was about to close my laptop when I heard the ping of an email. Quickly, I lifted the lid, and Chadwick's name appeared in my inbox.

Amber,

I've given up trying to reach you by phone, but do you know anything about this?

Forwarded email from:

Carlton Magma, CEO of Magma Industries.
We've bought this apartment in Hastings—see attached. Organize the

deed to be transferred out of Magma, Inc. and into the name of Amber Andersons' mother by COB today.

Carlton.

I let out a gasp. My skin tingled from my feet and up my legs. I should be angry, shouldn't I? He knew I wanted to do this on my own. He knew I didn't take help from anyone. *Why would he do this?* He owed me nothing. We owed each other nothing. Was it a parting gift knowing he'd soon be married off to his Bridezilla Celia?

As much as I wanted to feel angry at him, I couldn't bring those emotions to the surface. Confusion and chaos circled in my head. Did he expect me to thank him?

I pushed my head into my hands. *Oh God.* Of course, I'd have to thank him, but first, I'd have to accept his help. Something I thought I'd never have to do. But bit by bit, the walls I had built up around me were crumbling, and I think I was beginning to be okay with that.

What I had intended was to take a moment, drink my coffee, and think about what to say before calling him. It hadn't worked. In one hit, I downed it, the bitter taste hitting the back of my throat. Somehow thinking this through would only make it worse.

I clicked open my phone, clicked his name that I'd saved after our meeting him in the boardroom, and hit the call button.

"Amber."

Just hearing his voice, my stomach did a fucking backflip. "Logan…"

"How are you?"

"Fine, and you?"

"Amazing."

"Well, that's nice to hear," I said, laced with sarcasm.

"It's amazing to hear your voice," he said.

"Sure, it is." *Fuck. No, be cool, Amber.*

Silence echoed down the line. "Sorry. I just rang to say thank you. Thank you for buying my mom her apartment. God, who says that? It sounded so ridiculous."

"How did you find out?"

"My old law firm is handling the conveyance."

"Ah."

"I need to know… why did you do it, Logan?"

He exhaled. "Because I didn't want my family's stupid deal getting in the way of your bonus."

"But who buys someone a house?"

"And I care about you, Amber."

I swallowed. *Remember, he's practically engaged. Betrothed to another. You can't be the other woman.*

I pushed away the sadness threatening to take hold of my fractured body. *Compose yourself.* "Thank you." I cleared my throat.

"You don't need to thank me, Amber. You've done more for me than you know." I heard him suck in a breath. "And just so you know, I quit the family business. I am broke and happy to be. And there is no Celia, there never was."

There is no Celia. My breath hitched and held in my throat. "Why?" There wasn't any point hiding the fact my voice broke like an eleven-year-old boy.

"So many reasons, Amber."

The silence was deafening. My heart thudded, and my cheeks burned. *Amber, go on, tell him how you feel. Tell him you—*

"Maybe one day when I'm back in Queensland, I'll look you up and tell you all about it, but right now, I have a plane to catch." *You're too late.*

"Where is it this time? Paris, Hong Kong? Never mind, I'd like that, though. Friends?" The suggestion sounded so absurd as it rolled off my tongue.

He laughed. "Were we ever that?"

I sighed. And as much as it pained me, Logan had stolen a

piece of my heart, and I didn't have the courage to tell him I'd fallen for him. We'd missed our chance, and he was moving on.

"Bye, Amber."

"Bye…"

I hung up first, barely able to breathe. He wasn't engaged, and he'd quit. He'd found his voice and his own set of values and finally believed he could step out of his family's shadow, throwing his wealth to the wind.

I sat quietly in my armchair, thinking of what could have been. If I hadn't put on my armor suit, the one that guarded my heart, we might have been together. If we hadn't argued, and I hadn't pushed him away after Celia's arrival, things might have been different. If I'd taken a leap of faith and opened my heart to him, then he'd know how I truly felt about him.

But like moments in time, we had had ours. It shone brighter than the summer sun on a cloudless day, and it's warm and tingly feeling stayed with me, knowing I had those memories.

Maybe that's what love was. Wishing the man you love well, even though you know you're not meant to be together.

20

LOGAN

It wasn't Mykonos or Sardinia, but that didn't matter. If it was near her, I would have picked the shitty fly-in-fly-out cabin all over again. I would have taken it with both hands.

The beach crashed and billowed, its turquoise water swallowing the chalk-white sands. The street below me buzzed with tourists and locals. Even with the milder weather, beachgoers still flocked, and tourists lazily drank their Saturday afternoon daiquiris and margaritas.

I unscrewed the bottle of Evian, a better choice than the hotel's mini bottles of booze.

A last-minute booking didn't give me too many options, but I'd secured a standard room with a beach view. Quick to book out penthouses across the world when I traveled, this was different or maybe it was me who was different—a good different. As someone beautiful and wise once said, it's just a roof over your head. And I know, it's the company you keep that's more important than the size of the bed or the feel of fabric on the bedroom furniture. Funny thing was, this was perfect—

with a queen bed, white duvet, and comfortable fabric armchair I plonked myself in. Oak floorboards and a simple round table were the only other features in the sparsely decorated, yet refreshingly minimal room.

The cool bubbles of Evian slid down my throat, and I reflected on my conversation with Amber merely twelve hours ago.

The conversation went exactly how I thought it would. She had values, so I knew she would call. I also knew Carlton would pass the conveyance over to her old law firm, and she was tight with her old boss, so finding out was a possibility. But did I expect her voice to break? *Hell No. Not at all.* I knew there was a deep connection but hearing her on the line, her voice breaking then clearing to cover it, my stomach churned just as it did in those last days at the cabins with her.

I'd told her about quitting and being cut out of the family fortune, and I sensed shock down the line. But also, I knew deep down, she was proud. She believed in me enough for me to take that irrevocable step.

But then she couldn't. And I expected that too.

Even with her own voice breaking and feeling the way I knew she must feel about me, she still had her wall up. She'd leaned into her own walls like a safety behavior, a twin she couldn't part with. Until now. If I couldn't push her to let go and believe in love, then I wondered if she could ever feel it at all because the feeling she gave me was real, and I wasn't sure I could articulate it. Nonsensical feelings, swirling day and night, consumed my entire body and mind.

I exhaled and picked up my phone. Two hours until showtime. I stared at my reflection in the mirror. Was I nervous? *Yes.* But I couldn't afford to be.

My phone buzzed in my hand, and I turned it face up. *Mother* flashed up on the screen.

I left the house yesterday with my chest out and everything left on the table. On the plane, I received step-by-step documents on the staged repair of the mine. After realizing the date on it was from last year, the speed at which they got it to me was then no surprise.

It had been copied in the email to the head engineer of Danker Gold, detailing the action points and the company Magma had entrusted to complete the works. Also attached to the Heads of Agreement document for the merger were the details of the repair work.

My plan had worked, perfectly. So why was Mother calling now?

"Mother."

"Logan, darling, are you okay?"

I let out a laugh, but quickly reigned it in. *Since when had she ever asked me if I was okay?*

"I'm perfect, couldn't be better."

"I bet you could."

"What's that supposed to mean?"

"I've spoken to your father. Just your father, not your brother. For the record, I had no idea about the bribery and corruption going on with Senator Jones."

"And you're telling me this because…"

"I'm telling you this because I've put an end to it."

I laughed. "And how have you done that? Dad has never listened to you before."

"Simple, darling. I hold fifty percent of this company. And if he didn't listen, I was going straight to the board."

"Okay… well you've certainly got my attention now."

"So, Magma is still buying Danker Gold. Senator Jones is going to allow a minor acquisition of the land next to the mine… nowhere as big as your father and Carlton agreed to. And in return, the senator is keeping his money and his mouth shut. There will be no more Christmases with us, no more holidays."

"And how about the workers, Mom?"

"The workers will remain. They will repair the mine in the next three months. I'm overseeing that."

"You're working?"

"If you call that working. Darling, I helped your father make this company flourish. That's why I was never around during your childhood."

"But you were for Carlton's."

She sighed. "I haven't been the perfect mother, and I don't pretend I was. But I can make it right, now. Carlton and Dad will never cut off your inheritance. You are and will always be a part of this fucked-up family, Logan."

"That's the first time I've ever heard you swear!"

"Did you hear me, Logan?"

"Yes, but, Mother, can I ask you something?"

"Of course."

"I'd like to set up a charity arm for the business."

"What a great idea. Your father will like it too because of the tax breaks."

"Right."

"But I think that sounds wonderful. Give back to the little people."

"Ah Mother, let's not call them *little people*."

"Oh, right. Then I can help you, I can be the face. If you need to throw charity balls or raise funds… ooh, this sounds like a perfect mother-son plan. If you'll have me."

Heck, the woman was practically pleading. "Well, we can sort the details out later. But I'm interested in providing funds and support to miners who have to be away from their families, mainly one-parent families and families with sick children. Maybe help them fly in and out more frequently or even offer to pay for their family members' treatment altogether. Like this one guy, Jim. His daughter is terminal—"

"Done. Let's start with Jim."

Wow, well, all right.

"Yes, Jim. His daughter is terminally ill."

"Treatment sorted. Magma has it covered. Oh, this feels great!"

"Awesome, Jim will be stoked."

"Stoked?"

"Over-the-fucking-moon happy."

"Excellent. Now will you come over for dinner tonight?"

"Raincheck. I'm in Queensland, and to be honest, I'd much rather meet you at a café than that house. It isn't good for my soul."

"Your soul? Okay… I guess I could meet you at a restaurant, but what are you doing in Queensland?"

"Getting my girl."

She nearly choked on what was most likely her glass of sherry. "Well, I'd like to meet whoever has stolen your heart. So, promise me, you will come back soon and with the mystery girl."

"Sure. Wish me luck."

"You don't need luck, darling, you never have."

She sniffled and the thought of her welling up again took me by surprise. This new emotional and awakened mother had been vacant all my life, and now she appeared keen to make it up to me.

I guess I could start cutting her a little slack. "See you soon."

"I'd like that so much." She sniffled again, and this time, I had to hang up before I heard any more of the foreign sound coming from her.

Well, bowl me over with a wrecking ball. That came out of thin air. *Who was she, and what had she done with my mother?*

She was a confusing cat, but perhaps a leopard could change their spots, after all.

The tangerine hue of the sun dipped along the furthest edge of the ocean, the horizon a rainbow of cerulean blues and oranges as I sucked back the rest of my Evian. The only thing missing from this equation was my girl.

21

AMBER

If I had paid attention to Lily yesterday, I would have said no to dinner tonight. Being in a restaurant and making idle chit-chat with a group of women I hardly knew was not on my list of priorities. But being in the same restaurant where Logan cornered me with his sly arrogance and sexy-as-hell confidence had me wallowing before I'd even arrived.

Walking past the alleyway tore my stomach in two, and as I dipped my finger in the remaining chocolate sauce on my plate, the image of us under the sheeting rain was on loop. Vivid as it was weeks ago.

A blur of chatter surrounded the table. Before ushering Lily out the door yesterday, I promised to go to dinner with her. Even though it was with her group of floristry friends, she'd stressed she wanted me to be there, even if it was out of pity. It gave me a reason to shower, put makeup on, and shed the active wear that had seen less action in the last week than the Virgin Mary.

Lily pulled away from her conversation and glanced toward me, forcing me to plaster on a fake smile. I was happy for her. She had it all together, in love and right where she needed to be. Like I was happy for Jasmine in New York, but why couldn't I just sit in my pool of pity? Let me wallow over here while you are happy over there, I tried conveying back without words.

"Switch seats with me?" Lily said to Marley, her friend who'd been trying to make conversation with me all night. *Damn.* Obviously, the mind reading didn't work.

"What's going on, hun? You were okay when I picked you up, weren't you?" She curled her fingers around her chin.

"I'm fine." I lied.

"Uh-huh. Or maybe, you blindsided me with *that* V-neck bandage dress. By the way, those ankle boots are freaking amazing. I have to borrow these."

"Sure, anytime."

Lily tilted her head. "You're sitting here all pretty but totally glum. I don't get it. You had an amazing phone call with your mom yesterday. So, if I were you, I'd just call Logan."

Reluctantly, I stopped playing with my dessert. If I were alone, the plate would already be licked clean. It tasted like heaven on earth. But really, anything was better than the cardboard food I'd been grazing on all week.

"I can't do that, Lil."

"It's as easy as picking up the phone."

"You know my reasons."

"I think you can forget your reasons. Your walls are smashed to smithereens. He's torn them down. All you need to do is tell him you want him. I'm sure that's all he's waiting for. Didn't he basically say that on the phone?"

"No, he didn't say that. What he said was he broke it off with Celia and he had split from the family business."

"And you still want him?" She grinned.

I shook my head. "You know money has been more of an Achilles heel than anything for me."

"Damn straight. It's money that got you in this situation in the first place. Five years ago when you came to Seaview, you were only ever interested in making it on your own. Striving toward your own independence like an athlete striving for the Gold at the Olympic Games. So maybe… just maybe, if you hadn't set yourself up so rigidly in the beginning, you could have been open to having your own happily ever after."

"Lily? Hello? Can you pass the sweetener?" Sophie, her friend, cut through her monologue.

Lily grabbed the pastel pink packet and tossed it her friend's way.

"Everything has shifted since him."

"What does that even mean? Stop giving yourself these bullshit excuses. Do I need to dial his number? Is it even in your phone anymore, or have you erased him from your mind?"

"I've tried. But everything reminds me of him. It's just not as easy as I thought."

"Of course, it's not as easy as you thought. You fell in love, and you fell hard and fast. That just doesn't happen every day. Okay, it happened to Jasmine with a rock star, but it didn't happen to me. Heck, I had to have a do-over to get love right. Life is too fucking short, and—"

"Excuse me, ladies. I've got a round of our finest champagne for you, courtesy of the gentleman at the bar."

My skin pricked, my eyes widened, and my heart set off a new world record. *No!* I gasped. My chest pounded. I couldn't look around. Fear gripped me like a glove. With my back to the bar, I kept my gaze on Lily.

Her eyes widened as she zeroed in on the bar. "Oh, my. It appears we don't need to call Logan after all. Like a mirage, here he is, in Seaview, alone at the bar."

Blood flowed to my cheeks as the air vacated the vicinity. I whipped my head around.

I couldn't wait any longer.

I needed to see him.

I needed to believe he was here.

Our eyes locked, the hum of chatter disappearing as time stood still.

"Go to him," Lily whispered.

I wanted to get up and run to him like a scene out of a romance movie, but something still held me back. His piercing eyes locked with mine, and his lips curled into a hint of a smile.

My feet remained rooted to the floor, but I couldn't help but to return his smile.

"If I have to carry you, I will," Lily said.

22

LOGAN

From the dimly lit corner of the bar, I watched her. Delicately she fingered her dessert, licking her thumb and forefinger until she had me adjusting myself under the cloak of darkness. She sat, removed from the conversation of the girls she'd dined with, and only contributed with a nod or a smile now and then so as not to appear rude.

Amber sat, oblivious to the girls who wanted to be her and even more clueless to the giraffe-like males who craned their necks just to see her when they passed by her table.

Her dress clung to her hips like metal to a magnet. But there was nothing cold about her as she ambled between the tables toward me—not the warmth in her cheeks or the fire in her belly.

"You're here." Amber stopped a few feet in front of me.

"I'm here."

"Are you stalking me?"

"It's amazing what you can find out by someone's social media profile. Not yours, mind you. You've set your settings to private. Surprise, surprise. Lily, on the other hand, she's more open than Kim K."

"Did you really just compare my friend to Kim Kardashian?"

I grinned. Ah, I missed her. I missed this. "I did."

"Shouldn't you be halfway to Abu Dhabi by now?" She thrust out her hip, her saucer eyes regarded me.

"Take a walk with me, Amber."

Her gaze was alight with fear and fire. Her throat bobbed up and down as her focus flitted to her table, then returned to me. "I guess I can leave for a minute."

I dug into my jeans and found my wallet, producing a bill and palmed it onto the bar mat.

We walked toward the exit in silence, our steps fell in sync with one another just as I opened the door. As she walked past, her arm brushed my hand, and the cool exterior I'd walked in with left the building immediately.

A few more paces in silence, and we ended up around the corner in the same alleyway where it all started. Stamped in my memory, the desolate alleyway rose from the darkness from the single streetlight that shone above it. It's here, where we intertwined with our insatiable need for one another, the same place where her hands found their everlasting grip around my heart.

"Oh, no. Logan don't think—"

"I'm not here for that." I flashed her a wicked grin. "Although…"

Her cheeks bloomed a cherry pink as she pressed both hands into my chest, her forceful move doing little to set me off-balance. Instantly, I placed my hands on hers so she couldn't remove them, then pulled her close. She was close enough I could almost taste the sweetness of her dessert. "Ask me again, Amber."

She stood, unflinching, her hands clammy to the touch. "Why are you here, Logan?"

"You know why."

"I do?" Her sass reared its head again as I fully expected it would, but her mind and her heart were out of alignment. I gripped her hands tighter as they trembled beneath mine.

Tilting my head to the side, I drank her in. Finally, understanding the Amber that stood in front of me—her fears, her hesitations, her determination, and her unfathomable beauty.

Eventually, she opened her mouth to speak. "Maybe I do."

"Amber, I've realized a few things lately. The night we met we were both searching for something. You helped me realize I'm enough, even if my family doesn't think so. And second, money doesn't bring you happiness. I mean it helps… but living your own truth with your own values and sharing them with someone that's so frustrating and gorgeous, does."

She smiled and flicked her hair behind her ear. It fell forward and dusted her cheek. Naturally, I curved it around the shell of her ear.

"But I know you've realized a few things too."

"I have?" Her response weakened. The walls were crumbling just like I knew they would.

"You have. Deep down you know you're not to blame for your mother's situation. You held onto that because it kept you safe."

Her eyes appeared glossy, but she didn't waiver.

"You also realized that your rules, as inked as they were on your heart, were never designed to keep you safe. They kept you miserable. Once you broke rule one… never sleep with the same guy twice, you opened up to me like you've never done before. And by breaking rule two… never sleep with someone from work, you focused a little less on work and gave a bit back to yourself."

"Logan, please." She lost eye contact as she gazed to the ground.

Gently, I tilted her head, so she had nowhere to look but into my eyes. "No. I can't stop. You see, Amber, you've changed me, and I'm here to tell you, you can do the same." I exhaled. "But you're the one who has to jump. I can give you the parachute, but it's you who has to make the leap."

She blinked back the pools of water in her eyes. "What are you saying?"

"You're a smart girl, Amber." I couldn't do anymore. The next step was hers for the taking or not. I let go of her hands, and they fell to her side. Every fiber in my body screamed to hold her close, and it took every ounce of energy to do the opposite.

A tear rolled down her cheek, and I wiped it away with my thumb. I no longer wanted to be the source of her pain.

"I'm so scared, Logan," she whispered.

"I know you are, but I'm not. I want this more than anything I've ever wanted in my life. I want you, Amber, sass and all. I want you in your cranky, hangry moods, and I want you even when you don't want me. I'm going to be here. I'm not going anywhere. You know why?"

"Why?" She breathed.

"Because you deserve to be loved, and you deserve to let someone in and take care of you. Even though you're fiercely independent, know that I won't ever take that from you. Ever. I love that about you. Goddammit, I love you, Amber."

Tears spilled from her eyes as her entire body trembled.

"And if that wasn't enough, I can give you a hell of an orgasm."

A crack of laughter escaped her lips.

I waited for what felt like an eternity. My skin tingled, and my stomach churned. What was only a few seconds, felt like minutes had passed.

She held her hand to my face and stroked my cheek. "Fuck."

"Fuck?" I echoed.

"I love you, too, Logan." She closed the gap between us

and pressed her lips to mine. Her hands rested on the nape of my neck as I wrapped my arms around her waist and absorbed her kiss. A kiss under the sultry streetlight that tasted like candy wrapped in forever.

"For a moment there, I thought you weren't going to jump," I said, momentarily pulling away.

She grinned. "I had to keep you on your toes."

I widened my eyes. "Come here, you." I pulled her in closer this time, roughly chasing her lips with mine, my heart burning with a fire lit only for her. The ocean crashed and roared as the sky split into two with a flash of lightning.

She pulled away breathlessly. "Round two?"

A grin spread across my face. "You don't have to ask me twice," I said, enamored by the brazen beauty in my arms.

"Not here… I live a few minutes away." She beamed like a billboard on Times Square.

"You're insatiable, Amber Anderson."

"I'm never going to apologize for that."

"I would never want you to."

She winked, then grabbed my hand, and with a quick pace, started running out of the alleyway and toward the lit street.

EPILOGUE

One month later

So, when they say everything works out in the end, I guess I was skeptical. Who were *they* anyway?

But as I sat at the dining table of Mom's new home, things couldn't be more perfect. Mom washed up the dishes from the humblest of dinners, while Logan stood beside her, daffodil patterned tea towel in hand, drying them.

I can't help but wonder if *they* knew all along that things would work out.

Since the night I jumped, metaphorically, into his arms in the dingy alleyway in Seaview, things had yet to come crumbling down. I landed the Junior Associate role Chadwick had put me up for and was working my way up the corporate ladder.

Crighton's lawyers represented people who had little money to go against developers and governments making unjust claims on their land. And Rachel, my boss, was a mom of three who believed in work-life balance. So, forget sixty-plus hour weeks and hello flexible work with even a few work-from-home days.

As it turned out, I had all this free time—time to make love to the perfect man, both in the morning and at night.

And that was easy when distance was no longer an issue. Logan had moved from Perth to Seaview, and if I wasn't at his house, we tangled in the sheets at mine.

He'd purchased his own waterfront house. Not the obscene monstrosity that appeared like a monolith on the south end, but a small, 1960s beach shack with priceless views. He'd even decked it out with Parker furniture—I doubted they were replicas.

My ears pricked up when I overheard Mom bring up his new home.

"Amber tells me you've engaged an architect already, what are you planning?"

"I'm contemplating renovating versus rebuilding," Logan said.

"Renovate," I yelled.

He turned around, his hair falling over his eyes as he smiled with his perfect teeth.

I shrugged. "What?"

He turned toward Mom. "Does your daughter always get her way?"

"Always." Mom laughed, throwing me a heartfelt smile.

He returned the smile, and I wanted him to wrap his arms around me and trace me with kisses like he'd done just before we had gotten here.

"Well, if that's the last plate, I think we might call it a night. I've got to get sassy-pants home, then head to the mine early tomorrow."

Mom let out a giggle. "Good idea. It's getting late."

I frowned. I'd completely forgotten he was heading to Danker Gold tomorrow. True to his word, Logan had scheduled a meeting to verify the safety issues of the mine had been rectified.

I hadn't met his dad, nor seen his brother, Carlton, since the initial meeting in the boardroom at Chadwick Lane, and Logan hadn't seen or heard from them since arriving in Seaview. He certainly didn't care, and neither did I.

His relationship with his mother was getting better by the day, and more surprised than anyone, was Logan himself when she'd followed through on her word, keen to help him get the charity off the ground. In under a month, they'd not only helped Jim with his daughter but also eight other miners, providing financial support for their families in their times of crisis.

Proud was an understatement. The man in front of me was a frickin' rock star in his own right.

* * *

The drive from Hastings to Seaview was only ten minutes. I reached over the gearshift knob and rested my hand on his taut thigh as he expertly guided the car around the tight bends toward home.

"You know, you've won over my mom without even trying."

"I'm that good, am I?"

"Don't go blowing your own horn… it's still early!"

He chuckled. "Dammit, girl, I love you."

"I love you back." I giggled absurdly. This whole thing had to be a dream.

He slowed down, pulling the car over onto the side of the road. "What are you doing? Is there something wrong with the car?"

"There is definitely nothing wrong with the DB9, but there is something." His voice sounded off.

My heart began to thud. A million different thoughts rushed to the surface like subtitles in a foreign movie.

He was happy, yes. Was he sick? God, no. And surely, he wasn't going to propose. *Don't be absurd!*

He reached into his back pocket.

Fuck!

He held out his hand and opened it.

"It's a key." I exhaled, then sucked in a breath so I wouldn't pass out from lack of oxygen.

"Very observant." He placed the key in the hand I had rested on his thigh. "Amber, I want you to take another leap. Move in with me, please, I—"

I wrapped my hand around the key and pressed my lips to his, knowing in my heart there was absolutely zero leap to be taken. After a beat, we caught our breaths, and the fear in his eyes evaporated into happiness.

"It's not a leap, when it is meant to be," I said, bringing my lips to his once more.

THE END.

WHILE YOU'RE WAITING FOR YOU NEXT FIX...

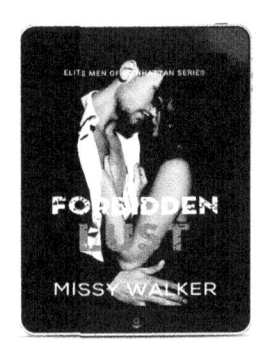

Have you started the popular Elite Men of Manhattan Series?

Dive into Book 1 Forbidden Lust, and get the first chapter FREE here...
https://BookHip.com/FMVHRXL

ALSO BY MISSY WALKER

Elite Men of Manhattan Series

Forbidden Lust

Forbidden Love

Lost Love

Missing Love

Small town desires

Trusting the Rockstar

Trusting the Ex

Trusting the Player

Join Missy's Club

Hear about exclusive book releases, teasers and box sets before anyone else.

Sign up to her newsletter here:
www.authormissywalker.com/newsletter

Become part of Missy's Facebook Crew
www.facebook.com/AuthorMissyWalker

ACKNOWLEDGMENTS

Inspiration for this book poured out of me in a matter of weeks. So a big thank you goes to Mr Walker for being on children duty and letting me write like a crazy woman undistracted with my headphones and supplying me with endless tea.

Vin & Cath thank you for your in-depth knowledge on mining and M&A.

To my fellow author gals; Jemma, Olga, Jenny and Selina, I feel like this journey would be a whole lot emptier without you in it. Our regular banter and advice is more than you know and I'm so thankful for it.

Missy x

ABOUT THE AUTHOR

Missy is an Australian author who writes kissing books with equal parts angst and steam. Stories about billionaires, forbidden romance, and second chances roll around in her mind probably more than they ought to.

When she's not writing, she's taking care of her two daughters and doting husband and conjuring up her next saucy plot.

Inspired by the acreage she lives on, Missy regularly distracts herself by visiting her orchard, baking naughty but delicious foods, and socialising with her girl squad.

Then there's her overweight cat Charlie, chickens, rabbit and bees if she needed another excuse to pass the time.

If you like Missy Walker's books, consider leaving a review and following her here:

tiktok.com/@authormissywalker
instagram.com/missywalkerauthor
facebook.com/AuthorMissyWalker
www.amazon.com/Missy-Walker
bookbub.com/profile/missy-walker

Printed in Great Britain
by Amazon